"My mother wants to see me happily married. But second marriages are harder to do right than first ones. I can't take chances with my kids."

"I agree completely," Eleanor said.

"You do?"

"Yes. Pete, I really like Cassie, but I'm not trying to use her to get to you."

"Now that's honesty. Thanks for saying that. I want you and Cassie to be friends. I just didn't want her to get hurt, you know, start thinking of some woman as more than a friend. Does that make sense?"

"Yes. But I know how much my Aunt Mavis added to my life. If Cassie forms a friendship with me, I won't let her down. Promise."

"I know this is a cliché, but can we just be friends?" Pete glanced her way. "I'm not looking for more than that now."

"Yes," Eleanor interrupted him. "We can be friends." This attraction would pass, but their friendship wouldn't have to—if she stuck to her antiromance guns.

LYN COTE

and her husband, her real-life hero, became in-laws recently when their son married his true love. Lyn already loves her daughter-in-law and enjoys this new adventure in family stretching. Lyn and her husband still live on the lake in the north woods, where they watch a bald eagle and its young soar and swoop overhead throughout the year. She wishes the best to all her readers. You may email Lyn at l.cote@juno.com or write her at P.O. Box 864, Woodruff, WI 54548. And drop by her blog, www.strongwomenbravestories.blogspot.com, to read stories of strong women in real life and in true-to-life fiction. "Every woman has a story. Share yours."

Building a Family
Lyn Cote

Love Inspired

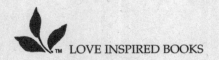

Recycling programs for this product may not exist in your area.

LOVE INSPIRED BOOKS

ISBN-13: 978-0-373-81578-4

BUILDING A FAMILY

www.LoveInspiredBooks.com

Printed in U.S.A.

Take therefore no thought for the morrow: for the morrow shall take thought for the things of itself. Sufficient unto the day is the evil thereof.
—*Matthew* 6:34

To Laura, a great knitter, lawyer and friend!

Chapter One

Under the intense June sun, Pete Beck parked his new blue pickup under a shady maple on New Friends Street in Hope, Wisconsin. "Here we are," he announced to his two teenaged passengers. Ignoring the negative vibes rippling from them, he slid out and folded his seat forward to help his exuberant four-year-old daughter Cassie out of her booster seat.

Under a blue, blue sky, he swung little Cassie up into his arms and kissed her cheek with a loud raspberry. She shrieked, "Daddy!" and giggled. The two teens climbed down from the truck and trailed after him, their hands shoved into their pockets. Pete experienced a flash of sympathy for the two teens. Maturing from a boy to a man wasn't ever easy.

Before he could stop her, Cassie squirmed and broke out of his arms, running ahead.

"Cassie!" he called. "Wait!" He raced after her. He caught up to her just as she halted in front of a tall African-American man holding a little girl about the same age as Cassie.

"Hi." Cassie waved up at the little girl. "Pretty. In your hair." Cassie pointed to the bright beads braided into the dark hair.

"You need to say thank you," the man said, letting his daughter down to join Cassie.

"Thank you," his little girl parroted, pointing at Cassie. "You got sunshine in your hair."

"I do?" Cassie looked upward at her own hair.

"Some people call her hair strawberry-blond," a soft woman's voice said from behind Pete.

He turned and saw Eleanor Washburn approaching him. She looked different than she had that bleak day back in March when they'd met. More relaxed. Even kind of pretty.

"I'm Kevan Paxton," the African-American man said, offering Pete his hand.

Pete shook it. "You're the family that's getting this Habitat house, right?"

Kevan grinned. "Yes, we're the lucky family—"

"I'm Cassie," Pete's daughter said to Kevan's little girl. "What's your name?"

"I'm Tiesha. My mama's gonna have a baby." The little girl rested her head on her mother's rounded abdomen.

"I gotta big brother. He's at Little League with my grandma."

The adults, who'd paused to listen to this exchange, chuckled.

"I'm happy you came," Eleanor said, holding her hand out to Pete. "Kevan, this is Pete Beck, the building-trades teacher at the local high school. And I see he's brought along two of his students."

Pete took Eleanor's hand, surprised to feel calluses on her palm. *That shouldn't surprise me. This is the third Habitat house project she's directed.*

The two teens, one on either side of him, nodded, then mumbled something. Both refused to make eye contact. Kids. They thought they knew it all, yet they had so much to learn.

Eleanor glanced at her watch. "It's time for me to get the dedication started. Kevan, will you bring your family forward so I can introduce you?" She smiled at Pete and patted Cassie's head, then turned and walked toward an area already excavated for the foundation.

Pete couldn't help watching her go, assessing her.

"She's why we didn't want to come," Luis, one of the teens, said under his breath, near Pete's ear. "We been in trouble, you know? She defended us in juvenile court so she knows what we did. I mean, it was just stupid stuff, but we got in trouble for it." Luis lowered his voice more, as if not wanting Cassie to hear. "That lady's down on us, man."

"All in your imagination." Pete reached down to take Cassie's hand. But she was running again. He hurried after her. How could little legs move that fast?

Eleanor took her place at the front of the crowd. A bee buzzed past her nose. She began her welcome. "Good morning!" she called out, holding up her hands.

The crowd quieted and turned toward her.

"I'm so glad you've come to the dedication of the final Habitat house to be built here on New Friends Street." She smiled with all her might, hoping her zeal would prove contagious. "I'd like you to meet our Habitat family." She motioned with her hand. "Kevan, will you please come forward and bring your family with you?"

Kevan grasped his wife's hand and led his family to Eleanor, Cassie tagging along. "My pleasure, Ms. Washburn." He faced the crowd, exuding happiness. "I'm Kevan Paxton. This little sweetheart is our four-year-old daughter." His little girl favored Kevan. "And this is my wife, my strength." With hair neatly beaded into corn rows, his wife looked happy, healthy—and very round. "As you might notice, another little Paxton is due to arrive in August."

Laughter punctuated the well-wishes called out.

Eleanor noted that the two little girls were holding hands. The sight of such innocent sweetness touched her deeply. "Thank you, Kevan," Eleanor said. "And thank you for your service in Iraq—"

Spontaneous applause and whistling broke out. When the applause ebbed, she started to speak about Habitat for Humanity. Kevan and his family moved away to stand beside Pete.

Then someone yanked her pant leg.

Eleanor glanced down to see Pete Beck's pretty little girl with her strawberry-blond hair. Cassie lifted her arms to Eleanor. The gesture was unmistakable; Eleanor's response was automatic. She swung the child into her arms—and felt herself swept up in brand-new sensations. She couldn't recall ever holding a child. The desire to have a child of her own coursed through her with startling force.

The little girl wrapped her arms around Eleanor's neck and hugged her. Then she leaned back and, nose to nose with Eleanor, said, "You're pretty."

More chuckles bubbled up from the crowd.

Eleanor couldn't speak. The child's innocent, impulsive gesture had wrapped around her vocal cords. And she loved the child's soft weight and chubbiness and strawberry-shampoo-scented hair. *I want a little girl of my own, Lord.*

Pete hurried forward, his arms outstretched. "I'm sorry. Cassie, you're interrupting Ms Washburn."

Cassie clung to her as Eleanor studied Pete's face. He looked chagrined. This loosened Eleanor's throat. "No harm done, Mr. Beck. She's no trouble." She looked at Cassie. "You can stay if you'll be quiet. You see, I need to talk to these people."

"I'll be quiet," Cassie vowed, her teeth denting her lower lip.

"You're sure?" Pete asked.

After both Eleanor and Cassie nodded, he returned to where he'd been standing with the two teens. Cassie's presence added a new zest to Eleanor's mood as she put her enthusiasm about the two previous Habitat houses into words.

The recipient of the first of these houses, Rosa Chambers, hurried over from Eleanor's yard a bit tardy and waved at her from the back of the crowd. All the while Eleanor talked, Pete's gaze never strayed from her face. Her face warmed not with the sun but from his attention. Could he be afraid that his daughter might say or do something embarrassing? She smiled at him, hoping he'd relax.

At the end of her talk, she urged, "Now, I need everyone who's interested in volunteering to give their contact info to our volunteer, Rosa Chambers, the recipient of our first Habitat house built last year."

She motioned to Rosa who—as planned— had gone over to a lawn chair in the shade of an oak tree and now sat with an open laptop. The crowd broke up. Some volunteers proceeded directly to Rosa; others stopped to chat. Pete and the two teens gravitated toward Eleanor. They hung back till the few people who'd stopped to exchange words with her moved away.

Cassie hugged Eleanor's neck again and then laid her head on her shoulder. The feel of the little girl in her arms broadened Eleanor's smile. And filled an ache within. How precious, this little girl. How lucky Pete Beck was.

She turned her attention to Pete, who must be in his mid-thirties, just a little older than she. Pete was good-looking, medium height, brawny build, with dark hair and eyes. The two teens, Luis, dark-haired and wiry, and Colby, blond and tall, flanked him. Her mind zipped back to more than one scene where these two teens had been her pro bono clients, defendants in juvenile court when she'd been their lawyer. Cassie babbled happily and quietly about the people she saw, waving to everybody from Eleanor's arms. A bee flew past Eleanor's ear.

Cassie squirmed to get down. "I want to go to Tiesha."

After Eleanor released her, Pete intercepted Cassie before she ran away. "Just a minute, Cassie. I need to talk to Ms. Washburn. Then we'll go see the little girl again."

Cassie frowned but didn't pout. Tethered by his hand, she twisted and turned, keeping track of the other little girl through the milling crowd of adults.

"I'm going to sign up, and I brought Luis and Colby to volunteer, too," Pete said, sounding as if he were measuring each word. "They just graduated and will probably only be working part-time this summer."

"Luis, Colby," Eleanor said, "you may go over to Rosa Chambers and give her your information. We'll be happy to use your muscle power for a good cause."

Luis and Colby looked to him. He nodded toward the young woman under the oak tree. The two of them loped away, grimacing.

Eleanor frowned as they walked off. Working here, helping others would be good for the teens, but these two might not be up to the challenge.

"I'll keep them in line."

His words were meant to reassure her. Yet he must be aware both teens had been designated "at risk." How could she handle this? While she appreciated his concern for these two young men, her goal was to build this house without delays. Two troubled teens could cause delays by misbehavior or carelessness on-site.

"I'll keep them in line," he repeated in a lowered voice.

"I'll hold you to that," Eleanor said quietly, but in her "courtroom" tone. Then she made the mistake of looking into Pete's eyes. They were a very deep brown. She caught herself staring into them a fraction of a second too long. She switched her gaze to Cassie, and her heart softened.

"I'll go sign up then, Ms. Washburn." Pete turned to go.

"If we're going to be working together, you should call me Eleanor, Pete."

He nodded and looked down at his daughter. "Okay, Cassie, we'll go see that little girl."

Cassie grinned up at him and then grabbed Eleanor's hand. "You come, too."

Pete's gaze met hers. "Please join us," he said, his tone somehow negating the invitation.

She flashed him a hesitant smile, wondering why and thinking she should really be mingling. But... "Okay."

As they walked, Cassie grasped her hand, connecting the three of them.

Eleanor noted people glancing at the trio they made and—speculating. She loved this small town, but life here could be suffocating at times. Eyes were always watching. She kept her chin up and hoped she wasn't blushing. Cassie broke away from both of them and ran to Tiesha. "Hi again!"

"Thanks for volunteering to help out," Kevan said to Luis and Colby, his daughter clinging to his good leg. "It's great to see you young guys reaching out and volunteering. Appreciate it."

Luis and Colby grinned and shrugged, obviously out of their depths.

"It's our pleasure to be of help. We're grateful for your service to our country," Pete said.

Kevan ignored Pete's comment on his military career but smiled down at the two girls.

Cassie pulled Eleanor closer to Tiesha. "This is Ella—Ella—"

"Why don't you girls call her Miss Ellie?" Tiesha's mom spoke up.

"Okay," Cassie and Tiesha said slightly out of unison.

The new title made Eleanor smile, feel wanted in a new and special way. She touched each girl's hair and smiled.

"You haven't given me your contact information," Rosa said to Pete with a smile.

"I'm pleased to meet you, Rosa," Pete said, quickly giving Rosa what she needed. She handed him the schedule which showed that work started toward the end of the week.

"It's time we were off," he said. Both Cassie and Tiesha had squatted to observe a busy anthill nearby. "Come on, Cassie."

"But I don't want to leave Tiesha," Cassie objected.

"Cassie, you'll see Tiesha again sometime soon—promise. We've got to take Luis and Colby to apply for summer jobs today." He motioned to Cassie to come to him.

Cassie looked unhappy but obeyed. She halted beside Eleanor. "Will you come and see me, Miss Ellie? I live on my grandpa's farm—"

The last of her words were obliterated by a motorcycle roaring up New Friends Street. Pete recognized that motor. He turned to watch his brother rock to a halt at the curb. A sideways glance told him that Eleanor, "Miss Ellie," looked uncertain. Did she equate "biker" with "trouble" like a lot of people?

Like mindless moths to a flame, the two teens broke into a run, heading for the bike.

His brother Mike climbed off the cycle and shed his gloves and helmet. The two teens flocked around him. He greeted them but, arm upraised, headed toward Pete.

Pete sent another glance Eleanor's way. He found himself gazing at three little freckles on the bridge of her nose. And the way her long hair moved with a breath of breeze.

"Hey! Pete!" Mike called out, unzipping his leather jacket, which sported a Harley Davidson patch. Six-foot-six with shoulders nearly as broad, Mike towered over his brother. He had a voice like a grizzly bear.

"You like to make an entrance, don't you?" Pete replied in a wry tone.

Mike just shrugged. "Such a sunny day! Couldn't waste it driving my pickup. Where do I sign up?"

A shrill scream shattered the peace. Pete swung around, his heart lodged in his throat. He recognized that voice. *Cassie!* Where was she? Why had she screamed?

Chapter Two

"A bee stinged me!" Cassie shrieked, waving her little arm. "A bee!"

Heart pounding, Eleanor raced right behind Pete to the child. Horrified, Eleanor watched Cassie's face turn beet-red. Was it just plain shock or anaphylactic shock?

"Is she allergic?" Eleanor asked. "Pete!" she demanded when he didn't reply. "Is she allergic?"

"She's…she's never been stung before." Pete swung Cassie into his arms and began running toward his truck.

"Stop!" Eleanor ordered, reining in her alarm. "If she's not allergic, we shouldn't go to the E.R." She paused for a steadying breath. "I have a first aid kit in my car. I have all we need." She waved him toward her dark green Trailblazer and forced herself not to run.

Still, she reached it first, opened the back hatch and laid out the soft, navy-blue blanket she kept there. "Lay her here." Eleanor's heart continued doing flip-flops.

Pete obeyed, resting his hand on his daughter's head, crooning to her soothingly.

"Miss Ellie," Cassie whimpered, "Miss Ellie, my arm hurts. A bee stinged me."

"Don't worry," Eleanor said as she opened the white plastic first aid box, people crowding around them, pressing close, too close. Feeling suffocated by their nearness, Eleanor waved them back. "I have everything I need to take care of you, Cassie," she said in a steady voice. "You're going to be all right."

"It hurts," Cassie said, breathing hard and fast.

"I know. I've been stung." Eleanor drew out the bottle of Benadryl spray. "This will help you." She held Cassie's soft, chubby, little arm outstretched and sprayed some on the sting, just below the elbow fold. Eleanor saw no evidence of a stinger, so it hadn't been a honey bee sting. Maybe a yellow jacket.

Cassie whimpered, holding her bottom lip with her teeth.

"Would you like me to give her some acetaminophen to help with the pain, Pete?" she asked softly.

"Yes." He hovered over his child, stroking her coppery-blond hair. "Do you have any children's strength—"

"I do." She opened the fresh bottle and poured a transparent purple dose into the tiny, plastic cup provided. Quaking inside, she forced her hands not to shake. "Now, sweetheart, this should taste just like grape jelly."

With Pete supporting her head, Cassie sipped it all and then shuddered with a heavy sigh. Pete let her head rest on the blanket again. Cassie's face began to look better, and she breathed without difficulty.

Pete exhaled. "I thought of the E.R. right away because I had a student who was stung, and he blew up in minutes. I just got him to there in time."

"I think Cassie is going to be fine," Eleanor said firmly to reassure the child. The little girl wasn't showing any signs of anaphylactic shock. Eleanor stroked Cassie's tear-wet face with a tissue, her own tension draining away, too. "Cassie, you're feeling better already, aren't you?"

Cassie let out another deep sigh and then nodded.

Eleanor whispered into Pete's ear, "You should watch her carefully for the next few hours, just to be sure."

Nodding, he accepted a blue, disposable ice pack and began to shake it so the chemicals would release the cold while Eleanor applied the antibiotic cream. "That takes care of it." Exhaling deeply drained away the last of her tension, leaving her feeling used up. "Whew. Too much excitement." She stepped back, pressing a tissue to the perspiration on her forehead.

"No!" Cassie objected, reaching for her. "Miss Ellie. I want Miss Ellie."

Eleanor reached for her hand. "You're going to be okay now. I promise."

"Want you." Cassie held up her arms to Eleanor once again. Eleanor looked to Pete for his approval. He nodded.

A deep emotion Eleanor had not experienced often swept through her, tugging at her. The desire to shelter and comfort this sweet child awed Eleanor. What had she done to deserve this? Stifling the urge to kiss Cassie's hair, she helped Cassie sit up. "You're a big girl—"

The abrasive roar of the Harley shattered the quiet.

Caught off guard, Eleanor cried out, "Oh!" and turned.

Taking advantage of the commotion, Luis had slipped onto the motorcycle and had started the motor.

Pete swallowed a few words better left unsaid. And ran flat out. Still, his brother Mike passed him.

"Turn off that motor!" Mike roared. "Get off my bike!"

Luis grinned and revved the motor a few more times. Just as Mike reached him, the kid cut the motor.

Mike pulled him off the bike. He relentlessly backed him up against the nearest, large oak tree. Luis stumbled on an exposed tree root, falling back and hitting the tree trunk. The force jerked the wind from him. The kid gasped and staggered to his feet.

"Don't you ever do that again." Mike placed one hand on Luis's chest, holding the teen against the tree trunk, not hurting him but preventing him from leaving.

Pete halted a few paces from his brother. Better to let Luis reap what his misbehavior had sown. It would pack more punch.

"Who do you think you are to mess with my bike?" Mike demanded.

"Hey, man," Luis said, trying to grin, "I didn't hurt the bike. I just wanted the feel of the bike, you know?"

With a fierce glance, Mike excoriated this stupid comment. "I know you're just a kid—"

Luis's face reddened.

"But you should know better than to get on

somebody's bike uninvited." Mike leaned forward, nose to nose. "And that motor has one hundred and twenty-eight horsepower and could have taken off with you. Then I'd have been left with a wrecked bike and you'd have been left just plain wrecked. No helmet. No leathers."

The teen began to look shaken. Pete stepped forward. "Luis, I think you should apologize to Mike."

"I'm sorry, man. I'll never do it again." Luis held up one hand as if he were taking an oath in court. "Never."

"Me, neither," Colby added in a thin voice nearby.

Mike glanced back and forth between the two teens. "My brother is probably way too easy on you two. But okay." He released Luis.

Freed, Luis slid down the tree trunk, caught himself and glared at Mike. Then he turned and stalked toward Pete's truck. Colby followed, running to catch up with him.

Mike pinned Pete with his gaze and then winked.

Pete shook his head. He turned to find Cassie back in Eleanor's arms. He didn't like the worried expression on Eleanor's face. Why had the kid pulled this stunt right here in front of her and half the town? But what could Pete do?

He'd have to watch these kids all the time—to get them through this summer and into the community college this August. He held out his arms to receive his daughter.

Cassie turned her face into Eleanor's neck and tightened her hold on the woman.

Already disgruntled over Luis, Pete prayed for patience. Today was only the first morning of the first week of summer break. *I must keep these teens too busy for mischief like this.* Earlier and again now, Ms. Washburn had made it clear with her words, voice and expression. She wouldn't put up with immature behavior from these two. The house came first with her. Luis and Colby came first with him. A tricky difference in goals.

"Cassie," Eleanor coaxed gently, "your dad is ready to take you with him."

Cassie shook her head, her face still buried against Eleanor's neck, and emitted a negative sound in the back of her throat. "Uh-uh."

Eleanor looked to him, lifting her eyebrows in silent query.

He pressed his lips together. How could he persuade Cassie away from Eleanor without a scene?

"I have a suggestion," Rosa spoke up. "Why doesn't Eleanor follow you to where you're taking the boys to apply for a job? She can perhaps buy Cassie a treat there? She's been such a brave girl."

The woman stroked Cassie's back. "Eleanor, I'll stay here and finish up getting all the contact info and giving out Habitat brochures and work schedules to volunteers. I'll bring the information to you later."

Now Pete raised his eyebrow, asking Eleanor for her opinion, not wanting to put her on the spot.

"I think that's a good idea," Eleanor conceded. "I was going to have to go into my office soon, anyway. Where are you going, Pete?"

"We're heading to Dairy Queen first and then A&W."

"I'll close up my hatch and follow you there. And, oh, I'll need Cassie's car seat." She headed toward her car.

"Okay. I'll get it for you. Thanks." He hurried toward his pickup.

"I'll close up your hatch," Mike offered.

Eleanor nodded and carried Cassie to the passenger side of her Trailblazer and opened the backseat door. Soon Pete hooked the booster seat in place, and Mike slammed the back hatch shut. Eleanor gave Pete a little smile and then settled Cassie in the car.

After hooking Cassie into her seat, Pete laid

the ice pack on her outstretched arm. "You be good, and I'll see you at Dairy Queen."

Cassie nodded and yawned. All the excitement had taken its toll. Pete walked away, hoping that this scene wouldn't repeat itself when Eleanor tried to leave Dairy Queen.

Why did complications keep cropping up? He'd had a simple plan to keep Luis and Colby busy this summer, do some good and take care of his family. Now, because of Cassie's instant liking of Eleanor, he'd have to handle that. He didn't want a pretty woman bobbing up this summer. *I'm not made of rock.*

Passing by fields of wisps of green corn seedlings, Pete drove toward the Dairy Queen on the state highway outside of town. The atmosphere in the cab of his pickup could only be termed sullen. Mike had stripped the cocky starch from the two teens. Both sat slumped with their heads down, not looking at him or each other. Pete kept his mouth shut tight, holding in prickly words. What had Luis been thinking?

Pete also wondered why Cassie had taken to Eleanor so quickly. Was it because she missed having a mom? The question shoved a sharp arrowhead into Pete's heart.

"You're really mad at us, aren't you?" Colby asked quietly.

Pete glanced to the right at them. "What do you think?"

"I don't know why your brother got so put out," Luis said, pouting like a four-year-old. "I didn't hurt his bike."

"If it was your bike—" Pete chose his words with care "—would you let just anybody climb on it without asking first?"

Luis shrugged and wouldn't meet Pete's gaze.

"Be a man," Pete barked, his patience snapping at this sign of stubborn immaturity. "Admit when you're wrong. You think you're fooling anybody?"

Luis's face reddened, and he tossed a resentful look Pete's way.

"You've got to grow up this summer, Luis. And you, too, Colby. If you let yourself think and act like you're still kids, you're going to get into *real* trouble. You're both eighteen now, and you won't go to juvenile court anymore. You'll be judged as adults, as men. You have to *think* before you act or…"

Neither teen replied. Pete fell silent again. He looked into his rearview mirror and glimpsed Eleanor's dark green Trailblazer. The big red Dairy Queen sign loomed ahead, and his tension tightened. Would these two teens make a mess of applying for jobs, too?

He pulled into the parking lot, bounded by

a Christmas-tree farm on two sides. The dash-board clock read 10:58 a.m. He'd hoped to get here earlier, before they opened for business. Without a word, the three of them got out and went to the employee's side entrance. Listening for Eleanor to arrive, Pete remained in the back-ground. Colby told the stocky, middle-aged, woman manager that they'd come to apply for jobs.

She eyed them, obviously assessing them. "You haven't worked here before."

"No, but we worked at the hot dog stand at the county fair the last four years," Colby replied.

"I'll still have to train you. Dairy Queen takes more know-how than merely handing people hot dogs." She turned toward a white-board scheduling chart hanging on the wall by the door. "You two can fill out applications, and then I'll call you to come and train. I'll tell you up front, I'm already full for the summer. But I can put you on the backup list. Somebody usually has to quit, and then I'll need someone. Okay?"

From the corner of his eye, Pete observed Eleanor arrive and park. Turning back to the teens, he grimly recalled his attempts to get these teens out to apply for summer jobs earlier.

Had Luis and Colby purposely avoided this so they'd be too late to get anything?

"There's your daddy," Eleanor said from behind him.

He turned to her. Cassie was holding Eleanor's hand. His daughter's face had relaxed, and her flushed cheeks has faded to normal. He opened his arms, but Cassie shrank back against Eleanor. He sucked down his exasperation. Cassie didn't usually behave this way. What had sparked this?

"Is it all right if I get her a baby cone?" Eleanor asked. "I don't want to spoil her lunch, but after being stung…" Her voice trailed off.

He dug into his pocket and handed Eleanor a few bills.

She waved the money away. "My treat. Would you like anything?"

As if on cue, his stomach rumbled.

"Let me guess, chocolate, large?" she said, grinning suddenly.

He grinned reluctantly in return and patted his waistline. "I'm not a teen anymore. Make that a medium."

Walking away, she chuckled and tossed him a smile over her shoulder.

When he turned back, Luis and Colby were filling out applications on clipboards. The intense concentration on both their faces caused

Pete to grin to himself. They didn't need him. He hurried to catch up with the ladies.

Soon the three of them were sitting down at a picnic table in front of Dairy Queen. Cars had already pulled up, and the lunch rush was on. Eleanor licked a vanilla cone and Cassie a much smaller, chocolate one. He began making short work of his own. He wished he could think of some small talk, but gazing into Eleanor's green eyes, his mind had gone blank.

"I think it's wonderful that you're taking an interest in Luis and Colby. They need a strong man in their lives," Eleanor said.

Pete shrugged. "They have potential."

She nodded. "I wish I could interest more teens in participating in the Habitat project. They have so much energy and could benefit so much from learning building skills. Are there any other of your students who would have time to help us out?"

"I hadn't thought about that," he admitted.

"Miss Ellie, do you got any kids?" Cassie asked.

Eleanor smiled but looked pained.

Pete wondered why.

"No, no kids," Eleanor replied. She looked as if she might say more, then her cell phone rang. Holding up one finger, she dug it out of her purse.

He watched her expression become serious. Cassie stopped licking her cone to gaze at Eleanor, too. He took a napkin Eleanor had put on the table and wiped Cassie's ice-cream face.

Eleanor snapped the phone shut and sighed. "This has been lovely, but I've been called in on a case. I have to go, Cassie."

"No—"

Eleanor caught Cassie's free hand. "I have to go, honey. Somebody needs my help so they don't go to jail."

"Jail? For bad people? Like on TV?" Cassie asked.

"Yes, Cassie. I will see you again." Eleanor rose, then reached over, touched Cassie's nose and smiled.

Pete stood, too. "Thanks for taking care of my girl. You know, with the bee sting." He offered her his hand.

She shook it. "I was glad I was able to help," she said, holding on to his hand, then releasing it abruptly.

Cassie looked downhearted. Pete rested his hand on her shoulder.

"Bye, Cassie. And Pete, please think over what I said about involving more of your students." Eleanor waved and headed toward her car. Her cell phone again to her ear, she walked briskly to her car.

Cassie's gaze followed Eleanor till her Trailblazer vanished around a bend in the road. Pete wondered what kind of case had come up.

"She looks just like my mama," Cassie whispered.

Pete dragged in air, shocked by these words. Cassie couldn't remember her mother. She'd left when Cassie was only an infant.

"Do you remember your mama?" he whispered, his heart punctured, bleeding.

Cassie shook her head. "Not my real mama, but the mama in my dreams. I dream about my mama sometimes."

Pete sucked in the moisture that sprang to his eyes. He didn't know what to say. How could he heal the hurt in his little girl?

That evening, Pete called in his son and daughter from the swing set near his parents' blue-and-white, two-story farmhouse. Seven-year-old Nicky clearly showed that he'd descended from the Becks, with his dark hair and eyes and sturdy, little body. Cassie favored her mother, willowy with reddish-blond hair.

The two raced in the back door, jockeying to reach him first. He herded them to the mudroom laundry tub to scrub their hands and faces. He watched them take the simple task and turn it into a contest of wills over soap, water and paper towels. Sibling rivalry. The everydayness of this soothed his ragged nerves. His daughter's words earlier that day had haunted him.

An earlier conversation with his brother had further unsettled him. Mike had called, saying he might need a favor. But before he'd said what he wanted from Pete, he'd rung off; a customer had come into his shop. Pete let out a long breath. Life never let up, did it?

Pete led his children to the long table on the screened-in side porch where the family enjoyed most of its meals in the warm weather. His mother didn't like air-conditioning. She'd gone green in the 1970s and never looked back.

Out here in the country, unhampered, cooling breezes blew most of the time. Also, a grove of tall, spreading oak trees, planted by his great-grandfather, shaded the farmhouse under its leafy, green canopy. A light wind stirred the leaves above, sounding like distant laughter. In the nearly ten years he'd lived there, he had missed open-air summers like this in one-hundred-plus degrees, air-conditioned, Las Vegas summers.

Tonight six of them sat down to supper, his family of three, his parents, Kerry Ann and Harry, and his youngest brother, Landon. A bowl of a tossed salad, more the size of a vat, another one of macaroni salad and grilled brats in homemade buns—yum, his mouth watered. His mother had set a place for Mike but it remained empty. Their two other brothers had married and only came when invited. But Mom always set a place for her unmarried sons.

With the sleeves of his plaid, cotton shirt folded up from his wrists, his father bowed his head and all followed his example. "Father, we are grateful for the food You have provided and for the hands which prepared it. Amen." His father's grace never varied and neither did its unmistakable sincerity. Shorter than any of his sons, his wiry father had been toughened by a life of hard work. And as always, his dad soberly thanked his mother for preparing another good meal.

The bowls began to make their way from hand to hand. Sitting on the other side of Nicky and Cassie, his petite mother, wearing a pink blouse and denim cutoffs, helped him serve the children. His brother and dad began talking about the family's dairy cattle and the day's work, two milkings and planting hay.

Pete let the peaceful conversation flow around him, grateful his parents had taken him and his children in after they'd returned from Las Vegas three years ago. Pete scanned the nearby road for Mike.

His mom gazed at Pete over the rim of her tall iced tea glass, obviously studying him. "Cassie showed me where the bee stung her."

"Miss Ellie took care of me," Cassie piped up and stretched out her arm to display the red welt. "See. It's getting better. It only hurts a little."

"Yes, Ms. Washburn took good care of you," he repeated, hoping Cassie wouldn't say more about the lady. "Now, more eating, less talking, please."

His mother searched his face. Aware that his mother was always listening for a sign of interest in any eligible female, he smiled deceptively at her and took another bite.

Landon, his tall, lanky youngest brother, home for the summer from University of Wisconsin Madison, spoke up. "I contacted the power company about the possibility of testing a wind turbine on our hill."

All conversation ceased and every eye turned to Landon.

"What did you say?" their father Harry asked, not sounding happy.

"You heard what I said, Dad," Landon said, grinning with his usual easy insouciance.

His dad sent his mother a disgruntled look.

"Yes, Harry dear," Kerry Ann said, patting her husband's work-roughened hand, "Landon takes after me." The contrast between his parents, his free-spirit mom and his stick-in-the-mud dad gave their family a certain zest.

Pete listened but his mind took a different route. He and his brothers were preparing a special surprise for their parents.

Thoughts of Eleanor returned. Unfortunately, Eleanor matched his ex-wife in two respects— both were beautiful and both were committed to their law careers. There was something different about Eleanor—but maybe that was just wishful thinking. *I have two kids to raise— that's my main job now.* Cassie's revealing words, about dreaming of her mama, had left him reeling. *I can't take any chances that might hurt them more.*

Pete heard the roar of Mike's Harley coming up the drive. Within minutes, Mike walked onto the porch, his hair wet from where he'd just washed his face and hands in the mudroom. He sat down at the empty place. "Hey, I made it!"

"This isn't a café. You should be here on time to eat your mother's good food," Harry grumbled, but he was grinning around his frown.

Mike laughed as if his dad had just told a joke. "Pass those bowls. I'm starving." Then he looked at Pete. "Hey, that Eleanor Washburn is one classy chick. Think she'd go out with me?"

Pete goggled at his brother.

Mike burst into laughter. "Just kidding. She's more your style, Pete."

Pete contented himself by just frowning discouragingly at Mike. From the corner of his eye, he glimpsed the expression on his mom's face. She was studying both of them with that motherly matchmaker expression. Not what Pete wanted at all.

His brother mouthed, "Talk to you later."

Fortunately, Landon started discussing the heavy rains and a waterlogged hay field. Pete began to relax. And then the image of Eleanor holding Cassie and tenderly brushing back wisps of her hair went through him in warm waves. This shook him. No woman had made him feel anything since Suzann had walked out on him and their two children.

He regained control of himself and concentrated on the farming discussion, while also wondering what favor Mike wanted and if Landon had made progress on finding a site for the large crowd to be invited for the surprise celebration they were preparing for their parents. Then Pete noted a dark green Trailblazer driving up to their house.

Eleanor got out and walked toward them. Surprised, he wasn't certain it was good for Cassie to see her again so soon.

He rose and hurried to greet her, trying to

figure out how to handle this. "Eleanor, what brings you here?"

"I'm sorry to intrude, but I couldn't get you on your cell phone, and the Habitat volunteer application didn't have another number for you. And there are so many Becks in the phone book."

He reached into his pocket and pulled out his phone. "Oh, my battery ran down. What do you need?"

"Pete, don't keep the lady standing there!" his mother called out. "Bring her over so we can offer her something to eat."

"Miss Ellie!" Evidently Cassie had finally recognized Eleanor.

Pete's heart beat like a trip-hammer.

Cassie leaped from her seat and ran to the woman, claiming her hand and drawing her to the table. "You can sit by me." Cassie pulled Eleanor to the place beside her. Pete trailed after them, trying not to give away his qualms.

"I'm so sorry to intrude on your meal," Eleanor apologized again. "I'll just stay a moment—"

"No, you can stay," Cassie said. "You'll like my grandma's food."

Kerry Ann laughed at this. "Have you eaten Miss Ellie?"

Eleanor gazed around. "No, I haven't but—"

"Won't take me a minute to get you a plate," Kerry Ann said, bustling toward the kitchen.

So within minutes, Eleanor had taken the place next to Cassie and was squirting mustard on her bratwurst. "Thank you so much. I haven't had a moment to eat since my ice cream cone at Dairy Queen with Cassie and Pete earlier today."

His mom had delivered everything Eleanor needed, and the bowls of food were passed to her. Pete watched her take a dainty bite of her bratwurst in its bun. Or she tried to take a dainty bite. Mustard squirted and then dribbled down her chin. He resisted the urge to wipe it away with his napkin. She finished chewing, and after swallowing, she gave an apologetic smile, dabbing off the mustard.

"What can I do for you, Eleanor?" Pete asked, unable to rein in his curiosity and his desire to get her on her way home. He kept an eagle eye on Cassie.

"You do know Danny Miller, right?" she asked. "You brought his brother this morning."

He wished she hadn't mentioned this here and now. Mike wouldn't want to discuss Danny Miller in front of their father—who had warned Mike not to hire Danny.

"What's Danny done now?" Pete's dad asked, looking disgruntled.

"Nothing," Eleanor replied. "I think it's just an unfortunate circumstance. He has been charged with vandalism and theft."

"The police took him from my shop today. Danny didn't break into those cars," Mike said. "He knows enough about cars to get one open without making a big mess, breaking windows and stuff."

Eleanor nodded, chewing macaroni salad. "But his fingerprints were found in the car." She turned to look directly into Pete's eyes. "Danny's mom is very upset, and she wondered if you'd come to court with her tomorrow morning. She's at work now, or she would have come to ask you herself."

"Me?" Pete lifted his tall glass of iced tea, taking time to consider. "I don't know what I can do—"

"You've helped her so much with Colby," Eleanor said. "She's been through a lot with her sons."

"That's what I came to ask you," Mike said, sounding earnest. "Please."

Pete nodded, feeling his spirits lower at the thought of entering a courtroom, something he hadn't done since his divorce proceedings. The memory sent a shaft of pain through him. "Okay."

"Thanks." Eleanor beamed at him.

Then out of the corner of his eyes, he glimpsed his mother gazing speculatively at him. He hoped she wasn't getting any ideas about Eleanor and him. Mom usually never meddled in her sons' romances or, in his case, lack thereof.

Eleanor savored the homemade meal at the long picnic table under the shady oaks. She recalled her nearly empty refrigerator. She also was glad to forgo the postage-stamp-size kitchen table where she usually sat alone with a small TV perched at eye level to keep her company—poor company.

At this long table, she and Kerry Ann were the only women. That must mean that Pete definitely was a single dad. That made Eleanor a touch sad. From what she knew of Pete and his family, she didn't think he'd seek a divorce lightly. She'd watched friends divorce and observed the pain they suffered. It was sad.

When Eleanor ate the last crumb of her meal, her waistband clung a bit snugger than usual. Had she really had two helpings of everything?

Cassie leaped up as if she'd been waiting for this moment. "Wanta swing?"

Eleanor chuckled, half in delight, half in response to the unusual request. "I'm sure I'm too big for your swing set."

"Not too big for the wooden swing hanging from the tree," Kerry Ann piped up. "I swing on it every summer day. Great exercise and fun, too."

Pete's dad shook his head at his wife, but Eleanor didn't miss the approving gleam in the dark eyes.

"I'm sure Eleanor has to be getting home," Pete said, probably offering her a way out.

But instead, he motivated her to stay and try this swing. "As a matter of fact," she said, "I'm done for the day. And I'd love to swing."

"Yes!" Cassie squealed. She claimed Eleanor's hand and pulled her along to a wooden swing hanging by sturdy ropes from a venerable oak. Nearby was an elaborate, wooden play area with swings, ramps, a slide, monkey bars and what looked like the bridge of a ship, wheel and all.

"Daddy and our uncles made this for us," Nicky, Cassie's older brother, spoke to her for the first time.

"It's wonderful," Eleanor said. The set was a child's dream. Her gaze strayed to Pete, who was in turn gazing at his little girl. Eleanor's heart pinched. She only recalled her father looking at her that way once—after she'd nearly died in a childhood accident. She swung her attention back to Cassie.

"Here's your swing," Cassie said, pointing to it. "Sit down, and I'll push you."

Eleanor felt a bit self-conscious but obeyed. Cassie gave her a gentle push. Eleanor swung forward about an inch.

"Daddy, you push her," Nicky said. "Cassie's not strong enough."

Cassie seconded this.

From behind, Eleanor felt Pete lean close, grasp the seat on either side of her. Instead of pushing forward, he drew her backward, his strong arms almost touching hers. She caught a whiff of his scent, a mix of clean soap and honest perspiration. Backward she went, like going up a ski lift in reverse.

She gripped the ropes and lifted her feet, pointing her toes, naturally remembering how to swing. Then he let out a breath and released her. She flew forward, suddenly free of gravity, a breeze funneling around her, her toes reaching for the sky. She laughed out loud. Her upward swing ended and she swung backward, remembering—just in time—to pull her heels back and pump her legs. She flew forward again. She laughed out loud again. And Pete's chuckle harmonized with her laughter.

Cassie called out encouragement, clapping as if she felt Eleanor's glee, too. Grinning, Eleanor lost herself in the motion, the moment, the freedom. Finally, she recalled who she was. She let the swing slow, and then Pete was there in front of her, grinning. Low sunlight caught in his thick hair, highlighting the dark brown. She forced herself not to reach out to touch it.

As she put her feet down, he offered her his hands. "It's fun, isn't it?"

She accepted his callused, capable hands, a hitch catching her breath. "And good exercise," she said, quoting his mother.

"It's time for me to get the kids ready for bed." Pete released her hands. Why did she sense that he wanted her to go?

Her joy ebbed. "I should be going then—"

"No!" Cassie cried out. "Please stay and read me a bedtime story."

"Yes, why don't you?" Kerry Ann seconded from a nearby, white Adirondack chair. "First, though, you two children go shed your dirty clothes in the laundry room, get your towels and hurry out to the shower. I'll get your pj's."

Eleanor tried to make sense of "out to the shower," but couldn't. She looked to Pete.

However, Kerry Ann did the explanation. "I have an outdoor shower set up. Keeps my bathrooms clean from all the summer dirt and mud." She hurried toward the back door.

"And it's more fun!" Nicky shouted happily, running after his grandma.

Pete led her to the back of the house toward a six-foot-long, unroofed structure with walls that ended about six inches above the grass. Walking beside him launched a funny flutter in her stomach.

Trying to look unaffected, Eleanor stood back and watched the children run inside fully clothed and then jog back out as if in a race, wrapped in clean towels. Both of them flew into the outdoor shower—a door on hinges automatically flapping shut—and then she heard a shower of water splashing and squeals of delight.

Pete leaned closer. "My mom had my dad rig this up when I was about ten. My dad and my brothers and I got so dirty, playing and working around the farm, she decided we should leave the dirt outside."

Eleanor was impressed and said so. She trained her eyes forward, but they strayed and caught Pete's strong profile. The twilight was flowing around them; a fiery sunset limned distant clouds.

"That's not all. Come here." Taking her hand, Pete led her to the other side of the shower. "See, the water from the shower goes down this shallow incline to her garden. So every time someone showers, the garden is watered."

She let him release her hand but missed the connection. "Wow. That's thinking green."

Within a few minutes, Pete's two children came out damp and smiling in summer pajamas and flip-flops. After Kerry Ann finished towel-drying Cassie's hair, the little girl hurried to Eleanor and took her hand. "Read me a story. Please."

Eleanor gauged hesitation in Pete's expression. And instantly, she understood. Cassie had shown a marked preference for her ever since they'd met this morning. And Cassie was without a mom. Strangely, Eleanor thought she knew how motherless Cassie felt—though her own mother was alive and well in Arizona. This stirred her desire to read to her. But she looked to Pete, asking his permission.

"Please," Cassie begged.

"Okay," Pete said, still reluctantly.

He had every right to try to protect his child from becoming too attached to her so she said, "Just this once. And just one story."

Pete sent them to a swing on the wide front porch while he ducked inside for the basket of books. She and Cassie sat on the swing. After Pete gave her the basket, he sat on a white wicker chair nearby, and Nicky climbed up on his lap.

The little girl snuggled up against Eleanor,

a rare sensation for her and one that filled her with resolution to pursue adoption. Cassie had chosen a book, called *Tell Me a Story,* where various animals were put to bed by their mothers. As she read, Eleanor felt Pete's daughter relax against her. Just as had happened this morning, the touch of the trusting little girl broke some emotional shield, flooding Eleanor with streams of sensations and emotions. Evidently, she needed to guard herself against becoming attached to Cassie just as much as Pete needed to guard his child.

As she read aloud, Eleanor had to struggle to keep all that she was feeling hidden. Her heart had melted into a warm maternal puddle. She had to hold back from revealing this. Without saying a word, Pete had put up a "No Trespassing" sign for her. At the end of the book, she made herself rise to leave. "This has been a lot of fun, Cassie. But I need to go home now."

"But—" Cassie started.

"—but we'll say thank you to Miss Ellie for reading to you," Pete spoke over his daughter.

Cassie looked pouty but said, "Thank you, Miss Ellie."

"Yeah, thanks," Nicky seconded. "You did good."

"And I'll walk the pretty lady to her car," Mike said, appearing at the bottom of the steps.

"Thank you," she said, hurrying to join him, casting a farewell glance to Pete over her shoulder and giving a final wave to Cassie. She inhaled deeply, trying to release her own marked emotional reaction.

The two walked silently to her Trailblazer. "Thanks for helping Danny," Mike said after he'd opened her car door.

"It's what I do." She got in and drove away, saddened somehow. Bereft. How many times as a child had she made up an imaginary big family of brothers and sisters and a mom who was always in the kitchen, baking something which smelled wonderful? She sighed and turned onto the county road. Life was life— period. She might never have a big family, but soon she might find a child who needed her. She had love to give, meeting Cassie had proved that to her. Maybe this had been her sign to proceed.

Upstairs, Pete sat on the side of Cassie's twin bed. Nicky crawled into the other. He yawned loud and long and then asked his usual question, "Do we really got to go to bed now? It's not even dark yet."

"That's because it's summer. And yes, you still got to—" he paused to correct himself "—*have* to go to bed now. Prayers," Pete prompted. Both children folded their hands and bowed their heads. They said in unison, "Dear Jesus, take care of Grandma and Grandpa and Daddy and all our uncles."

"And Miss Ellie," Cassie added. "Thank You, Jesus, for all our blessings. Amen." They ended slightly out of sync.

Pete leaned over and kissed Cassie's fore-head, then stood and kissed Nicky's. He lowered the window shade, blocking out the sunset. Low in the sky, the summer sun's globe flamed gold-red, heralding another hot day coming to-morrow.

"Good night, kids. I love you," he said, his usual final good-night. Bountiful love for his children expanded within him as it usually did at this quiet time of the day, free of distractions.

"Good night, daddy. We love you," the two replied together.

"Daddy, when can I see Miss Ellie again?" Cassie's question stopped him at the doorway.

The mention of Eleanor caught him around the throat. The feel of putting his arms around the lovely woman as he hoisted the swing flashed through him. He cleared his throat. "We'll see about that. Now go to sleep." He walked out, only half shutting the door. He headed downstairs.

He hoped that Cassie would soon forget the

pretty lady at the "Happytat" site. But what would he do if he couldn't shake Cassie's fascination with Miss Ellie? Cassie's words at the Dairy Queen still repeated in his mind. Did her unexpected attachment to Eleanor have anything to do with Suzann's complete absence from her daughter's life? The last thought stung—worse than any yellow jacket.

Chapter Three

Glancing around the century-old, oak-paneled courtroom, Pete swallowed down a fresh, cold wave of gloom. Ever since his divorce, he hated courtrooms.

"I can't thank you enough for coming, Mr. Beck," Mrs. Miller repeated once more. The plump, dark-haired woman in a white blouse and navy-blue slacks looked to be about a decade older than he. On the wooden, pew-like bench, she perched beside him, wringing her hands. Unusually quiet and staid, Luis and Colby sat, both hunched forward, on his other side. "I'm so worried that Danny won't be going home with me today."

Not knowing what to say, Pete replied with a sympathetic sound.

"I just hope that your brother Mike doesn't... let Danny go because of this. Danny's had his problems, but he wouldn't steal anything." Mrs. Miller wiped away a tear.

"Mike says he knows that Danny didn't do it." Pete wished this whole thing would just get started, and that thought shamed him. He'd accepted that Mike couldn't come because he had to keep the shop open. But now Pete grasped why Mike had begged him to go to court with his employee's mom. This poor woman was beside herself. He softened his voice. "That's why he asked me to come. He wanted to show his support for Danny."

Mrs. Miller nodded, trying to look brave, but her lips trembled. "It's hard," she said, "raising boys without a father."

It's hard raising kids without a mother—the lonely thought echoed within him. He knew he was in the minority but the number of single dads in the United States was on the rise—unfortunately. He glanced sideways at the woman beside him. She looked older than her years, and from what he knew, she had worked two jobs most of her life to support her two sons.

This centered Pete, drawing even more of his sympathy. This woman hadn't run out on her two boys. She'd stuck with them. Not like his ex who'd left and never looked back. Mrs. Miller deserved his support. He touched her sleeve. "I'm sure Danny will be fine."

She smiled tremulously at him.

Then from the corner of his eye, Pete saw Eleanor stride confidently into court. Seeing her now jolted him. He'd only seen her in casual work clothes before. Here she wore a gray, three-piece pantsuit and carried a leather briefcase, very professional.

A flashback to divorce court, where Suzann had marched in with her colleagues and proceeded to destroy their marriage and abandon her children, set his teeth on edge. He tried to put a damper on it. Just because Eleanor and Suzann were both lawyers meant nothing.

Eleanor paused beside Danny's mom. "Mrs. Miller." She offered the woman her hand. "Don't worry, okay?"

Mrs. Miller nodded and squeezed Eleanor's hand with both of hers. "Thanks," she whispered.

Pete's gaze and Eleanor's connected. He saw the warm sympathy in her eyes. "And Pete, thanks for coming."

He nodded, uncomfortable in being thanked for doing something so small. And uncomfortable at noticing how good she looked here in a setting he so disliked.

High heels clicking, Eleanor went forward and sat at a polished oak table gated off from the general seating, her back to them. Only a few rows separated them. Eleanor had twisted her long hair into a tight bun low on the back of her head. He tried to ignore the fact that he couldn't take his eyes off the ivory nape of her neck.

Mrs. Miller leaned over and said, "Danny has a job this time, so he couldn't get a public defender. But Ms. Washburn didn't charge me both times she defended Colby. And she told Danny that he was an adult, so she would charge him. But he could pay her in installments. She's so kind."

"Yes, she seems like a nice woman," he replied inadequately. A very nice woman.

"All rise." The bailiff's sonorous voice woke up the courtroom. The sparse gathering rose. The judge entered and took the bench. The few people in court sat again.

Pete listened to the brief preliminary hearing. Danny pleaded not guilty, and the judge set a court date a month away, and after a brief discussion, set bail. Then, after Danny was led out of the courtroom, Eleanor rose and headed toward them. That was it? All this tension generated for less than five minutes of action?

Eleanor paused to speak reassuringly to Mrs. Miller. "Mrs. Miller, I don't think you or Danny have a lot to worry about. You need to go to a bail bondsman, and Danny will be released."

"Thank you so much," Mrs. Miller replied. "I know Danny didn't steal anything."

"Pete, thanks again for providing moral support. And you, Luis and Colby." She inclined her head toward the teens bunched behind him as if for protection. As Pete and the others proceeded up the aisle, he thought he caught just a whiff of Eleanor's perfume. He shook this off. *I have no business noticing anything. Romance is not something I'm ready for now or maybe ever.* After being discarded like yesterday's trash, how did a man get enough guts to give his everything to someone? And he couldn't think of just himself. He couldn't repeat the disastrous experience and by doing so, multiply the bad consequences to his children.

Later, as Eleanor hurried through her back door, she slipped off her heels, picked them up and nearly ran to her bedroom. What she had been anticipating for over a year had become reality today. Mavis Coldwell, PhD, the woman who had really raised her, had moved to town. Eleanor couldn't wait to see Mavis, her honorary aunt.

When she reached the bedroom, she quickly shed her professional shell and tugged on her worn blue jeans, green Hodag Music Fest T-shirt and slid her feet into her Birkenstocks. "Ahh."

Pete's kind face from their earlier court-room meeting flickered in her mind. Why had he looked so uncomfortable? Then she recalled yesterday, how tenderly he'd looked at Cassie. He certainly loved his children.

Brushing away a twinge of loneliness, Eleanor stopped in the kitchen and grabbed a six-pack of bottled green tea with honey and ginseng and then, off the counter, a box of vanilla sandwich cookies. She'd skipped lunch. She ran to her car and drove off east toward the best thing that had happened to her in a long time.

Within ten minutes she pulled up and parked beside Mavis's cute, little white Craftsman bungalow, with green shutters and roses blooming along the drive. Mavis met her at the front door. Her milk chocolate face split into a huge smile. "Ellie honey." She folded her soft, rounded arms around Eleanor.

Eleanor had to fight back tears of joy. She hugged Mavis tight against her, so happy to be reunited. "Aunt Mavis, I'm so glad to see you here for good."

"Me, too, Ellie." She looked at the box of cookies and the bottles of tea in Eleanor's hands. "Did you eat lunch?" she asked sternly.

Eleanor gazed around at the familiar furniture in Mavis's new home. "No, but I'll just—"

Mavis scolded her with a frown. "That ginseng won't make up for your lack of nutrition. Come in the kitchen. I've got leftovers from lunch. I tried that Chinese restaurant you told me about. Boy, did they give me food."

Grinning so hard she felt her face crinkle up, Eleanor followed Mavis through the small living and dining rooms to the kitchen in the rear. Eleanor sat at the small, round table just big enough for the two of them that Mavis had moved from her house in Madison. Like a little girl again, she'd come to Mavis's house where she would be made to feel special.

"I can't believe that I'm really here," Mavis said, spooning rice and what looked and smelled deliciously like almond chicken onto a dinner plate, "and for good, at last."

"It has seemed like a long process." Many months had stretched out while Mavis sold her home in Madison and looked for a house to retire to here, near Rhinelander.

Thoughts of Pete, flashes of his expression, suddenly bombarded Eleanor. *Stop,* she ordered her mind.

Mavis set the plate in the microwave over the stove and pushed On. "Well, the movers arrived this morning and by lunchtime, they'd moved in all my furniture. I just finished unpacking my kitchen stuff, and I need to unload a few boxes and suitcases of clothing."

Eleanor listened but Pete Beck with his serious brown eyes and the way his hair curled up behind his ears intruded. She brushed him aside again.

"After that, I'll unpack all my linens," Mavis continued. "I think I'll take my time about deciding what art to put on what walls, but I think I'll feel pretty moved in and settled by the end of the week."

Eleanor's unruly mind brought up the set of Pete's broad shoulders, and how it had felt when Cassie hugged her and told her she was pretty.

The microwave bell dinged, bringing Eleanor back again, and Mavis removed the plate and delivered it to Eleanor. She sat down across from her and sighed. "So far, I love retirement."

Eleanor chuckled and picked up the chopsticks Mavis had put beside her plate. She dug into the fragrant almond chicken and rice. "Yum. Thanks."

Pete Beck popped back into her mind. Cassie, bee-stung, in his arms, he was running toward her. Why couldn't she stop thinking about him?

"Is that what a Hodag looks like?" Mavis asked, pointing at the bizarre creature outlined in white on the faded, green T-shirt.

"Yes." Eleanor spread her arms so that Mavis could see it more clearly.

"Kind of like a cross between a dinosaur and a big croc," Mavis mused. "Weird."

"True, but when you're a little town in Wisconsin, you need something clever to use as a symbol. The Hodag's fun." Eleanor savored the salty and savory Chinese flavors, keeping her mind off Pete, barely.

"Your mom and dad will arrive in a few weeks for an extended break from the Arizona heat. *Quid pro quo.* I intend to spend a part of this coming winter with them in sunny Arizona. And after teaching at Madison for over forty years, we know we can get along."

Eleanor smiled, masking her mixed emotions. She wanted to see her parents, loved her parents. She only wished her mother felt the same about her.

"So what's on your mind?" Mavis asked. "You keep zoning out on me." Mavis lifted one eyebrow.

Eleanor felt herself go pink.

"Ah, a man."

Eleanor primmed her lips. "I am not dating anybody. You know how that always turns out." Evidently she didn't possess whatever it required to prompt a man to fall in love with *her, not* her resume and yearly income. "Two failed engagements are more than enough for me."

Mavis rested a hand on Eleanor's arm. "Just because two couldn't see what a gem you are doesn't mean all men are blind."

Pete's hesitant expression from last night came to mind. Maybe that explained why he intrigued her. He had probably been burned, too, and wasn't looking for love, either. *Good.* "You stayed single, Auntie."

"Not because I wanted to," Mavis declared, "but because I never met a man I wanted to spend my life with." The older woman fell silent a moment as if remembering. "A few men proposed to me, but never the right one." Mavis removed her hand and looked pensive.

Eleanor wanted to ask, "Were you ever in love?" She decided not to. Mavis loved her, but she'd always been a private person, even with Eleanor.

Mavis smiled. "Eat your food, honey. Then I'm dragging you outside to help me plant my kitchen garden—chives, cilantro, basil, sage, tomatoes, cukes and zucchini."

"Yum. I mean, only if I get to eat them, too!"

"Of course, I'll share." Mavis's expression sobered. "Enough about all this surface stuff. I want to know, have you come to a decision, then?" Mavis asked her, looking deep into Eleanor's eyes.

"Yes, I'm going to begin the process of adopting a child from the foster care system. I have an appointment with a social worker this week." Just declaring this out loud made Eleanor breathless. However, the memory of Cassie's hugs gave her courage. *I can do this, love a child.*

Her aunt looked serious but said nothing more.

Eleanor again began eating her late lunch. And when Pete Beck's face flickered in her consciousness, she blinked it away. Even thinking of romance and Pete Beck in the same sentence would be foolhardy. She forcibly pushed the man out of her mind. But the sensation from his pulling back her swing last night shivered through her once more. What a lovely family he had. Did he know how lucky he was? But soon she'd have a family here: Mavis, herself and a little daughter.

Noting the clouds flying in from the west, Pete drove up to the Habitat site where he and the two teens would work this morning. A few days had passed since the dedication. Later, he'd take a break and deliver the teens to Dairy Queen for training. A dozen or so people milled around the foundation that had been poured a few days ago.

His mother's face popped once again into his mind. When he'd looked back as he drove away this morning, she had looked thoughtful, perplexed. Had he let on that he'd been trying to get away without Cassie asking where he was going? That was more than he wanted his mom to guess.

Turning his thoughts to the present, he easily picked out Eleanor in the crowd. She stood tall enough that the top of her blond hair was visible over the other women. He mentally scolded himself for seeking her out. He had no business thinking thoughts about a woman. He turned his attention to Kevan Paxton, who stood beside her.

"Pete!" Eleanor called out his name and motioned for him to join her. "Pete!"

"What can I do for you?" he asked, meeting her beside the yawning foundation. After greeting Kevan, Pete schooled his expression to polite attention. Eleanor wore another of her plaid, short-sleeve shirts and crisply pressed jeans. In spite of the warm temperature, she appeared cool.

"Well, experience tells me that today we should be setting the sills and floor joists." She motioned toward a stack of raw lumber and boxes of nails and several hammers. "Would you take over and do the explanations?"

"Sure." He realized he'd propped his hands on his hips, a gesture of impatience or irritation. He knew that from a psych course on body language, and he knew it was pointed at himself, not her. He lifted his arms instead. "Everybody, let's get started!"

The crowd turned toward him. Luis and Colby hung back but did focus their attention on him. Ever since the day in court with Danny, both kids had been subdued. He hoped this meant that his warnings about growing up and keeping out of trouble were hitting home.

"Okay. How many of you have ever set a floor joist?" Pete asked, raising his hand.

A few hands went up.

"You with some experience, come forward, so I can hook you up with those who need guidance," Pete said.

The clouds overhead thickened and flew faster. He sent a worried glance upward. The crowd shifted, and three men along with Luis and Colby joined him at the front. He quickly learned their names. Then he let them help him show how to apply the sill and set the joists. "Luis and Colby here just finished building their first house with me at the high school, so if you can't get me, ask them."

Both Luis and Colby looked startled by his designating them as in the know. But if he wanted them to act like men, treating them like men could only help.

Work started.

Pete roamed through the groups of workers, giving pointers and encouraging them. He did it now as second nature; it was so similar to his job. Nine months of the past two years, he'd taught teens how to perform the different construction skills. He eased right back into teaching mode.

Except he couldn't stop himself from tracking Eleanor, as if she were on his internal radar, and tracking the gathering storm. The local weatherman had warned of a front, but much later today. An early rain would wreck today's work on this house.

"Sorry I'm late, Eleanor!" A woman's voice carried over the other voices.

Pete turned to see a tall, formidable-looking, African-American woman with large glasses heading straight for Eleanor.

"Aunt Mavis! That's okay," Eleanor said, smiling. In fact, Pete had never seen her smile so widely before. Who was this Aunt Mavis? He was curious in spite of himself.

The two women, dressed very much alike, embraced, and then they quickly started carrying floor joists together, one at each end, showing their strength.

"Pete!"

The familiar female voice stopped him in his tracks. He turned to see his mom and Cassie, holding hands, approaching him. "Mom! Hi! What's up?"

"Miss Ellie!" Cassie dropped her grandma's hand, racing for Eleanor.

Pete leaped forward and intercepted Cassie. "Whoa, whoa, honey. Let Miss Ellie get that floor joist in place. Then you can talk to her. This is a building site, not a playground."

His mother reached him. "Cassie," she scolded, "what did I tell you before we got out of the car?"

Cassie looked down at her flip-flop sandals. "You told me to hold your hand and not let go. That people are working here with nail guns and stuff."

"Are you sorry?" Kerry Ann asked. "And promise not to forget again?"

"Yes, Grandma."

"Okay, then you're forgiven. Take my hand." She looked at Pete. "Your cousin, Susie, took Nicky to ball practice—" she glanced up at the gray clouds "—and she'll drive him home in case of rain." Kerry Ann sighed. "Cassie and I won't stay long. I just wanted to see this Habitat project up close. I missed the first two."

Done with setting the floor joist, Eleanor came over to Cassie. She knelt on one knee. "Hey, there, Cassie. How's your arm?"

Cassie unfolded her arm, revealing the healing sting. "See, it's getting all better."

Kerry Ann moved closer. "Hello, Eleanor."

After returning the greeting, Eleanor turned to Mavis, who stood at her side. "This is my honorary aunt, Mavis Caldwell. She's just retired and moved here from Madison." Thunder sounded in the distance, and Eleanor looked concerned.

Kerry Ann smiled and offered her hand to Mavis. "Nice to meet you. Welcome to Hope."

Pete stood there, looking up at the sky, wondering how long before it rained.

"Thank you. I'm a little tired from the move but exhilarated by the work here."

Kevan came over. "Hey, who are these new ladies?" Pete introduced the three. Mavis shook hands with Kerry Ann and Kevan.

"What are your interests, Mavis?" Kerry Ann asked. "Maybe I can hook you up with someone who shares yours. And we have a senior center in town where there are congregate meals, if you're interested."

"Well, thank you." Mavis beamed. "I've already stopped at the library, got my card and signed up for a book club."

"Excellent. I'm too busy in the summer to read as much as I'd like, but I do the book club in winter."

Kevan wished Mavis well and returned to his job.

Pete continued hovering, listening to this, hoping his mom would finish and head home. He wanted to prevent another bonding experience between Cassie and Eleanor from occurring. It wouldn't be good for Cassie. Eleanor was not a part of their lives and, after this house was done, would no longer be around. He couldn't set Cassie up for another loss.

"Why don't you two ladies go sit on the lawn chairs in the shade and chat for a moment?" Eleanor suggested.

Pete's jaw tightened at this invitation.

"But I came to work," Mavis objected.

"You can take a break," Eleanor said. "Pete and I can work together. Go on."

Pete did not appreciate this suggestion, but how could he refuse? His mom, Mavis and Cassie walked over to the lawn chairs provided for those who needed to take a break.

Eleanor moved closer to him as they walked to the stack of floor joists. "That's really nice of your mom to be so welcoming to my aunt."

"I've got a nice mom."

"You're lucky, then."

Pete cocked an eyebrow at this odd comment. But he didn't ask what she meant. They arrived at the stack of wood. He lifted one end of the joist, and she lifted the other. Then he was walking slowly backward toward the foundation. Though thick, fast-moving clouds blocked the sun, perspiration had begun to collect around his hairline.

Eleanor glanced up. "I think that front is moving in faster than expected."

"Are you prepared for it, if it hits?"

"Yes, that's my job." She sighed. "But if it doesn't hold off, that will shut us down without much accomplished today." She then began calling out encouragement to the other volunteers, urging them to work as quickly as possible.

He and Eleanor, along with the others, soon had the sill and joists in place. Out of the corner of his eye, he glimpsed Jenelle Paxton and her little girl park at the curb and walk to the lawn chairs to join his mom, Mavis and Cassie. He heard his daughter's squeal of joy. She hugged Tiesha.

He'd have to be cut out of stone not to be happy for Cassie. She'd hit the jackpot today— Miss Ellie and Tiesha and now Mavis doting on her. The two girls began playing with some little Fisher-Price figures in the wild grass.

"Don't they look sweet with each other?" Eleanor murmured from close beside him.

He turned, and her expression caught him by surprise. Her tender heart shone through her eyes and the soft smile that touched her lips.

She frowned, suddenly looking pensive. "Cassie's mother doesn't live nearby, does she?"

"She couldn't care less about her children." The ugly words plopped out of his mouth and twisted his stomach.

Eleanor looked shocked. "I'm so sorry. That must be hard."

He didn't want to talk about this, but he'd added more. He changed his tone. "We manage. My parents help me."

Eleanor tilted her head to one side as if trying to see him in a different way. "I'm glad you have help. And you have a lovely mother."

He nodded. And more thunder, not so distant now, rolled, echoed in the distance.

"Oh, dear, the storm's upon us," Eleanor complained.

"We can't take any chances," he said.

"Right. We've got heavy-duty tarps to put over the raw lumber joists so they don't suck up the rain. Would you get everybody together and show them how to spread and secure them?"

He sent her a questioning look. She was turning leadership over to him?

"I'd like to spend a few minutes with Cassie. Is that all right?"

"Sure." What else could he say? "Are those the tarps?" He pointed to a stack of large, blue plastic squares still in their wrappers.

"Yes, and there are bricks and rocks to hold them down." Eleanor started away from him at a trot.

The wind was already whipping up. Tree branches swayed. Another storm was nipping them, moving into action. Pete called out instructions and soon the volunteers swarmed around the tarps, opening the cellophane wrapping and unfolding them. In pairs, they stretched the tarps over the foundation and unused wood. Then they positioned the bricks and rocks to hold the tarps down in the growing, buffeting wind.

By the time this was done, the first cold raindrops plopped around Pete's head and shoulders. He hustled toward his mom with Kevan close behind. "We should get you two on the road home."

"Pete, Mavis has invited us, including you and the Paxtons, to come to her house for an impromptu lunch," his mom replied, rising from the lawn chair and snapping it shut.

Excusing himself from the lunch, Kevan kissed Jenelle goodbye and headed off for his part-time job.

Pete realized that he would have to explain to his mom why he didn't want Cassie becoming so attached to Eleanor. The Habitat house would be built by fall, and then Eleanor would no longer be a daily part of their life.

"Pete, these lawn chairs belong to Eleanor," Kerry Ann continued. "Would you carry them to her Trailblazer and load them in her rear hatch?"

Again, what could he say? He nodded, hiding his frustration. Luis and Colby helped him snap the lawn chairs shut, and through the increasing rain, they hurried to Eleanor's SUV. She had the hatch open and was standing under it for cover from the pelting downpour.

"I'm going to drive Luis and Colby to Dairy Queen." He raised his voice over the din from the storm. "They're supposed to train there today. Where's Mavis's house?"

Eleanor told him the address. He ran straight out for his pickup, Luis and Colby right behind him. Inside the warm cab, he steamed physically from the rain on his wet skin and mentally from how the day had betrayed him. He'd had two fixed purposes today—to work at the Habitat site with the teens and to keep Cassie away from Eleanor. He'd succeeded at one and failed at the other.

Was his mom just being nice to Cassie and Mavis, a newcomer? Or was she trying to get him and Eleanor together? Since his divorce, his mom hadn't been the matchmaking or plotting kind of mother. But that appeared to be changing.

Chapter Four

Thrilled that Aunt Mavis hadn't wasted any time getting to know people, Eleanor wanted to be a part of the luncheon. But she hadn't missed Pete's hesitation at this invitation. Thinking over meeting Kerry Ann the other evening, Eleanor wondered if Pete's mother was into matchmaking. Was that why he'd hesitated over coming here today? That—or was this about Cassie? She tried to put herself in Pete's place.

Under a black umbrella and these swirling questions, she hurried to Mavis's back door, thunder booming in the distance. On such a gloomy day, she usually would have gone to the office earlier than expected. Now she ran up the three porch steps and entered the snug kitchen. Cheerful chatter greeted her and lifted her heart. Outside, the leaden gray skies poured rain; inside, every light downstairs shone bright. Lightning flickered at the windows, unnoticed.

Kerry Ann and Mavis were looking into the fridge and discussing the impromptu lunch menu. Mavis bent to pull out her large freezer drawer. "How about ham sandwiches and potato salad?"

"That sounds yummy," Eleanor said. "Do you have deli potato salad, or should I offer to peel potatoes?"

"I boiled potatoes and eggs last night," Mavis said. "I planned to invite you for a cookout tonight." She pointedly looked toward the rain pouring down the windows like someone outside held a hose to the panes. "Scratch that."

Eleanor shrugged. "I need to go into my office later today to catch up on paperwork. But I'll help—"

"Why don't you go into the living room where Jenelle is watching the girls?" Kerry Ann suggested. "She can probably use a hand."

Again, Eleanor hesitated for a second. Should she do this? Earlier in the week, Pete had shown subtle signs that he didn't want Cassie forming an attachment to her. Or that was what she had thought his body language had broadcasted. *I could be wrong about that.*

"Go on," Mavis said, waving her hands toward Eleanor. "You know you don't really want to be in the kitchen."

Squeals from the living room beckoned. Eleanor shrugged and followed the sound. Jenelle sat on the couch with Mavis's large marmalade cat on her lap. Tiesha stood on one side of Jenelle with Cassie on the other. Both little girls were petting the feline.

Jenelle looked up. "I've rarely seen such a laid-back cat."

Eleanor knelt down by Tiesha, subtly distancing herself from Cassie. "Dabney's great, isn't he?" She stroked the long cat who was stretched out like a baby. Dabney opened one eye and purred more loudly in greeting for a few seconds. Eleanor rubbed her nose into his soft fur, murmuring her affection.

"I've been wanting a cat," Jenelle said, "but Kevan and Tiesha have been talking dog."

"I want both!" Tiesha said, bouncing on her toes.

"I got kittens in our barn," Cassie said. "And we got golden retrievers that live in a big doghouse. But they can't come inside except in the winter. Then they sleep on the back porch."

"That's because we live on a farm," Kerry Ann added from the kitchen doorway. "My husband says animals don't live in the house."

She made a funny face. "But I love the old grump." She turned back to Mavis.

"How are you liking Hope?" Eleanor asked Jenelle. She wondered when Pete would get here. Maybe he'd call his regrets?

"I like Hope. We didn't want to return to Chicago after Kevan got back from Iraq. We wanted to move out of the city. Kevan had met a few soldiers from this area. Kevan came up and stayed with one of them and went around applying for jobs. He got picked up at the paper mill, and we're very grateful."

"I grew up in Madison," Eleanor said. "That's not Chicago-size. But after I got out of law school, I came here to be one of the county's public defenders to get courtroom experience. I liked it and set up my office here for good."

Someone was knocking on the front door.

"Get that please!" Mavis called from the kitchen.

Eleanor hurried to the door and threw it open, wondering how Pete would behave.

Pete didn't wait for an invitation. He rushed inside and stood, water dripping down his face. "I'm nearly soaked to the skin."

"Come to the bathroom," Eleanor said. "I'll give you a towel to dry yourself with." Eleanor led him to the small bathroom and gave him a fresh towel. She left him there and joined

Jenelle and the girls in the living room. She sat down beside Jenelle, and immediately Cassie climbed onto her lap.

That cozy sensation swept through her, the same cozy sensation that she'd experienced the first time she'd lifted Cassie into her arms. Eleanor didn't have the heart to discourage her. What could Pete do to her, after all?

Jenelle was reciting a fun rhyme with hand actions. "No more monkeys jumping on the bed."

Eleanor watched the repeating rhyme and joined in. The girls were giggling. Eleanor took a deep breath. She tried not to think of all the work waiting for her back at the office. She could work this evening. This was too much fun to miss.

Pete, still with damp hair, joined them, just sitting and listening to the females. Soon the impromptu lunch had been set on the dining room table. Eleanor tried to eat her meal, trying to ignore how Pete watched her and Cassie like an irritated hawk. Did he have to make it so obvious that he didn't want his daughter getting attached to her?

At the end of the meal, Pete rose. "I need to go pick up Luis and Colby." He hesitated.

Eleanor could almost see the cogs turning

in his mind. He was asking himself how he could get Cassie away from her. Suddenly irritated with him, she stood. "I'll walk you to the door. You may borrow one of the umbrellas and return it to me the next time I see you." What could he say?

He thanked Mavis for lunch and bid everyone goodbye.

In the small foyer, Eleanor whispered hotly, "I'm not going to encourage your daughter to become attached to me. *But* I think if you keep making a big deal out of it, you'll just make her more determined."

Pete looked as if he was chewing on a reply, but finally he merely nodded. "Okay."

Eleanor didn't want to beat him over the head, so she just nodded, too. "See you at the Habitat site on the next workday?"

"Right." He opened the door, opened the umbrella, and then his cell phone rang. He halted and answered. His expression mixed glad, surprise and caution. He hung up and shut the umbrella. "Luis and Colby are working today. Two kids that were scheduled didn't show."

"Well, that's good, right?"

He nodded. A new round of thunder pounded outside. "I guess I can stay."

"I guess you can." Despite his agreement,

Eleanor didn't know if she was happy about this or not. Would he lighten up or continue giving her the discouraging eye?

When they joined the group at the table, Pete sat down, murmuring he didn't need to pick up the teens. Then he stopped speaking abruptly and stared upward.

Eleanor, along with everybody else at the table, followed his gaze. She saw the problem immediately. A wet line had formed on the white ceiling toward the little chandelier, which looked original to the house.

"Did you have a home inspection, Mavis?" Pete asked.

"I bought the house as is," Mavis admitted. "I guess the county just let the old woman who owned it finish her days here. She was a couple of years behind in taxes. And now I see that I must have a leak, right?" Mavis sighed.

Eleanor worried her lower lip.

At that moment, what appeared to be a tear dropped from the chandelier and plunked onto an empty plate.

"Uh-oh. I better go up and see where the leak is," Pete said, rising. "Where's your access opening?"

Mavis led him to it, with Eleanor trailing behind, worried. Jenelle and Kerry Ann kept the girls at the table. Pete pulled down the cord to the trapdoor in the small hallway. With the opening of the hatch, an ancient, drop-down stepladder appeared automatically.

"That doesn't look very substantial," Eleanor murmured.

"It'll hold me." Still, Pete tested his weight on each step. Then he disappeared up into the attic.

Eleanor moved closer to Mavis, and they both craned their necks toward the dark hole above.

"Bulb must be burnt out," Pete called down. "Got a flashlight?"

Mavis turned and hurried into her bedroom off the hallway. But when she moved to put a foot on the bottom step, Eleanor intervened. "I'll go up, Auntie."

Mavis looked momentarily disgruntled, and then handed the large lantern flashlight to Eleanor. "No comments about those old stairs not holding my weight, girl."

Eleanor chuckled, snapping on the flashlight and ascending the rungs. As soon as her head cleared the floor, she peered into the near blackness of the attic. Flashing around the light, she illuminated Pete's feet in soggy Nikes.

He reached down and pulled her up. "Shine the beam at the roof."

Standing now, she did, aiming the light at the old, wooden beams and joists section by section.

"There." Pete touched her elbow. "Let's get a closer look." They minced along, balancing on top of the floor beams, not stepping on the raggedy insulation that lay between each. "There," Pete muttered.

Eleanor saw the wet mark on the weathered wood above their heads and the dripping water coming in. "Oh, dear."

Pete took the flashlight. "We need something to catch the drips in." He raised his voice. "Mavis, hand us up a few large pans to catch the water!"

"Oh, no!" Mavis wailed from below.

But within a few minutes, from the hatch, Eleanor was accepting a large sauce pan and a turkey roaster. "Which one do you want?" she asked Pete.

"Both. Here's a second leak."

Mavis grumbled something and then must have left the hallway in disgust.

Pete pointed the light onto another section of roofing. Then he shone the light so Eleanor could walk over and position the pans where they were needed.

Thunder exploded overhead. The faint light shining up from the hatch flickered and went out. Tiesha and Cassie, below, squealed with fright. And then the flashlight flickered off. Instinctively Eleanor reached for Pete.

He pulled her closer and whispered, "Just don't move. The lights will probably come right back on."

So they stood motionless, listening to the rain pounding against the windows. Thunder hammered overhead. In the darkness, Eleanor became aware of Pete's steady breathing and the warmth of his hands on her arms. She fought the urge to move even closer. She knew logically she didn't need his protection. There was really no danger. But she wanted to be nearer to him, his palpable warmth and strength.

Mavis's voice came up from the area below the steps. "We're okay. I got candles lit down here. Now I wish I'd bought that generator someone suggested. I'll come up and hand you my other flashlight. It's small, but it will help." She did this, shining the light over to where they stood.

Pete let go of Eleanor's arms. "I don't see any more leaks. We can go down now."

She missed his touch immediately and rubbed her arms, as if they were chilled. However, the attic was in fact stuffy and muggy. They moved over the narrow floor joists till they reached the hatch.

Pete motioned for her to descend first. She handed him the flashlight so she wouldn't leave him in the dark. She stepped down carefully as he trained the light onto the stepladder. And then Pete followed her down.

Mavis met them in the hallway. Before she could say anything, Pete announced, "I'm going down to the basement to check for water."

Mavis's eyes widened. "Oh, no."

"Just checking," Pete said, walking at a clip through the dining room into the kitchen and then down the basement stairs in the back hall. Eleanor hurried after him, keeping within the circle of light from the flashlight he was carrying.

"Mavis!" Kerry Ann called from the living room. "Come sit down. Let the young people take care of matters. Pete knows what he's doing."

Mavis must have obeyed, because she didn't follow Eleanor into the basement. Eleanor halted at the bottom of the rickety, open wooden steps into the basement, mentally making a note that they must be closed-in for Mavis's safety and a new railing installed.

"She needs to have the stairway made safe," Pete said, voicing her thoughts.

"I agree." She moved forward cautiously. He

was flashing the light toward the floor drain. She saw the wet trickle. "Oh, no."

"It's not bad." Pete swung the light toward a window. The window well was full and water was seeping through the seams around the glass. "This is just an especially bad downpour, much more than usual."

"So this is just because it's a bad storm?"

"Yes, but when the weather is better, I'd like to come over and check on your aunt's drainage."

For some reason, this comment hit Eleanor as hilarious. She tried not to laugh but it came out anyway in a burst.

"What did I say?" Pete asked.

"Checking…my aunt's…drainage," she managed to say between laughs.

"I get it." Pete flashed the light up on his face to show her he was smiling. "Enough of this frivolity—we need to make sure that there isn't any water oozing from any other place." He walked slowly around the small basement with Eleanor at his side, playing the light over each window and over each wall. Everywhere else looked dry. "Good. We can go upstairs now. That trickle isn't too much for the drain to handle."

He directed the beam of light at the steps and Eleanor preceded him up to the kitchen. She led him into the living room where Kerry Ann and Jenelle sat with the children and Mavis. Candlelight drew them through the dismal, low light, making Eleanor shiver as if gloomy storm clouds were wrapping themselves around her, around them all.

Pete swung around two dining chairs, and they sat under the wide arch between the rooms. A candle set on the table had been lit, along with one on the mantel, and two hurricane lamps flickered from their positions at each end of the couch.

Eleanor sat back and sighed as if she'd been working hard at the Habitat site. This afternoon had followed a different course than usual. She glanced at her wristwatch.

"Need to be at work?" Pete asked softly.

She shrugged. "I always have work to do. But this is kind of nice to be inside out of the storm."

"Thanks, Pete, for checking things out," Mavis said. "What's the bad news?"

"You don't have enough insulation up in the attic," he said, nodding at her thanks.

"I was going to ask you about the roof leak first," Mavis said wryly. "Don't give me all the good news in one big lump."

Pete grinned, looking a little abashed. "Sorry."

"So I have a leak in the roof?" Mavis held up one finger. "And—"

"Make that two leaks, Auntie," Eleanor said.

"Two leaks," Mavis groaned and held up another finger. "And not enough insulation." Another finger rose. "What else?"

"Pete needs to check your drainage outside," Eleanor forced herself to say this with a straight face, but a laugh shook silently inside.

Pete's mouth became a flat line—whether because he, too, was trying to hold back laughter or not, she couldn't tell. "I think I should go over the whole house and see what repairs need to be done. This is the time of the year that you should get these things taken care of. Not having a building inspection before buying is the pitfall of buying a house at a county auction," Pete said.

"I know," Mavis said. "People warned me. But honestly, I fell in love with the house at first sight. I've always liked these classic bungalows. And I loved the yard with all its perennials—"

"That probably need major thinning," Kerry Ann inserted with a chuckle.

Mavis let her hand fall. "Oh, well. It's only money and some elbow grease. And before this, I had enough work to do, getting everything basic fixed up so I could move in. I had to have all new electrical and have all the floors refinished and all the rooms painted."

"Well, if your basic systems are in good

order, that's a big plus. But I'll come over and go through the house inside and out to see if there are any other repairs are needed."

"What do you charge?" Mavis asked.

Pete looked surprised. "You don't need to pay me. I do this for friends all the time."

"Then you should be charging your friends," Mavis said. "I know what teachers make. And why should you give away your expertise?"

Pete shrugged. His cell phone rang. He pulled it out and spoke a few words. He rose. "Gotta go. The guys are done."

Eleanor rose, too, and walked him to the door. "Here. Take this." She handed him a plain, black umbrella from the stand near the door.

"No, that's okay. I won't melt."

They stood a moment staring at each other. The sensations Eleanor had experienced in the attic within his protection shivered through her. She shook them off. "Take care."

He looked at her as if he wanted to say something important, but instead he replied, "You, too." He opened the door and raced through the rain to his pickup. He flashed his lights at her and then drove away through the downpour.

Turning back, Eleanor stood in the doorway, gazing at the group, but thinking about Pete. How his hand on her arm had felt. How peaceful she'd been in that moment, how secure.

Eleanor sat down and Cassie crossed the room and climbed up on her lap. Holding the child had become so natural. She knew Pete didn't like it. But children needed love from people other than their parents, didn't they?

That evening, after Pete shuffled down the stairs, he went in search of his mom. They had something that needed to be settled, and now. He found her loading the dishwasher.

"I could use some help," she said brightly.

He grimaced out of habit but willingly started rinsing dishes and then sliding them into place in the dishwasher.

Kerry Ann hummed as she wiped down the kitchen stove and counter. "I like Eleanor. She's got a good heart."

This made it easier for him to bring up what he'd come to say and harder at the same time. "I like Eleanor. But I don't want—"

"You don't want Cassie becoming attached to her."

He looked up, startled.

"My goodness, at Mavis's table you were broadcasting it so plainly that any idiot could have read the message. I was almost embarrassed in front of Mavis. After all, Eleanor is like her daughter." She went on the offense then. "What's wrong with Eleanor?"

"There is nothing wrong with Eleanor. It's just that my kids have been through enough—"

"Cassie came to Wisconsin barely a year old. She doesn't remember Suzann at all."

Pete ignored this. "She has you."

"Yes, as her grandma. She wants a mama, just like any child does."

At this remark, he stilled. Salt in a wound didn't come close to explaining the pain that suffused him. A fire in his middle flamed out making it impossible for him to speak.

His mom came close and rested a hand on his arm. "Pete, you've suffered a great deal. But that has nothing to do with Eleanor Washburn. Cassie should not suffer because of the past."

"I don't want her hurt." *More than she is.* Guilt twisted through him like barbed wire.

"Then don't try to fight Cassie, let her like Eleanor."

"Eleanor is a busy woman—"

"Not too busy to help others. Mavis and I are taking Jenelle, Tiesha and Cassie to the library story hour later this week. I'm not going to avoid either Jenelle or Mavis just because they are associated with Eleanor."

Before Pete could respond, his mom continued, "I've wiped down the counters. Please start the dishwasher when you've finished." She left the kitchen.

His stomach burning, Pete finished the chore, pushed all the right buttons and controlled himself so he didn't close the dishwasher door hard. He walked into the living room and sat down on the couch to watch some TV show he had no interest in.

He couldn't contradict his mother. First of all, she was his mother, a good mother, a wonderful mother. Second of all, when he'd come back, she had welcomed him in—without any comments about his poor judgment in choosing a mate. Unlike his dad. And maybe his mom was right. Maybe he should let Cassie love Eleanor. Still, it felt wrong. Like stepping into the dark without a flashlight.

Later that week on Friday morning, Eleanor waited for the volunteers to gather. The Habitat house was coming along; the shell now stood on the foundation. Today they would begin sheeting the outside and, if time permitted, raising roof joists.

Would Pete Beck come? Or would he decide to stay home and avoid her? Last night as she thought over the rainy afternoon at Mavis's house, his attitude over Cassie liking her had started rubbing her in a very wrong way.

Kevan got out of his car and headed straight for her. "Morning, Eleanor!"

She couldn't have stopped herself from smiling back at him. This man certainly had a positive outlook. "Good morning! I think we're going to have a good turnout today."

"Hope so. Jenelle really enjoyed lunch at your aunt's house."

"Mavis enjoyed having her and Tiesha."

"We got some good news. My uncle Dex is coming for a visit." Then Kevan made a face. "But I think that Jenelle's got that matchmaking look on her face."

Eleanor glanced at him.

"Uncle Dex is around your aunt's age, a bachelor and another veteran. Vietnam."

Eleanor chuckled. "Well, that should prove interesting."

"That's one way to look at it." Another volunteer drew Kevan away to talk.

Pete's blue pickup pulled up and parked by the curb. Pete, Luis and Colby got out and walked toward her.

Eleanor lifted her chin, ready to deal with Mr. Beck's disapproval. Then she saw his face, and her sympathy flowed toward him. He looked worried, upset. Was this about her and Cassie again? Or something new? *Pete, what's wrong?*

Chapter Five

"Hi, Pete," Eleanor greeted him.

Looking into Eleanor's pretty face, Pete tried to soften his expression. Her genuine greeting had flowed around him like a soft breeze. But now she was frowning slightly. Clearly she had picked up on his frustration. How could he help that? He and his brothers had been blocked at every turn. If they couldn't find a place to hold the party for their parents, they couldn't pull off the surprise celebration. He swallowed his frustration. Right now, working on this house for an Iraq veteran should be center stage as his goal, not the party.

He forced a smile. "Good morning! Looks like we're having a rare sunny day."

She took a step toward him.

Luis and Colby, both wearing cutoffs and tat-tered T-shirts, ran up behind him. "Hey! We're here! What's on for the day?"

Pete swallowed an unexpected chuckle. Luis sounded like this was the place to be. What had caused that change in attitude? He eyed the two teens.

"Sheeting walls and raising the roof joists," Eleanor replied.

The day began. Pete kept an eye on the teens. As he carried another piece of sheeting to nail to the studs, he glimpsed Luis helping another volunteer with how to use the pneumatic nail gun. As he walked past them, he overheard Luis repeating to the woman Pete's own instructions about safety. A rare feeling of accomplishment warmed Pete.

Still, as he worked, he kept chewing on the fact that his brothers and he had struck out. Who knew a person had to plan a party a whole year in advance?

The day passed with some volunteers leaving and more coming. He focused on what his hands were doing, not on his frustration. Finally, Pete looked around. Where had everybody gone? Only he and Eleanor remained. His spirit reached for her, seeking her gentleness, her kindness. Comfort.

She approached him as if he were a booby trap that—without warning—might spring.

That irritated him. But then she was a woman, and one who obviously noticed things. Hadn't she nailed him on not wanting her getting close to Cassie?

"I think it's time you put away your tools," she said in the "after five o'clock" quiet he hadn't noticed till now. "And tell me what's bothering you."

"Huh?" he replied, displaying his lack of astute comprehension. He cringed at this dumb response.

"I've watched you work with a determination and focus that—by the way—moved the building schedule along at a faster pace today." She grinned. "You had the other volunteers hustling to keep up with you. Don't get me wrong. I'm glad so much was accomplished today, but it's obvious you're upset about something. Is it Cassie and your mom going to story hour today with Mavis and Jenelle and Tiesha? Though why that should upset you is a mystery to me."

The day's fatigue slammed him; the starch drained out of him. He needed to sit down. He waved his arm toward a wood bench set against a broad oak tree on the property. She followed him and sat down. He lowered himself and rested his tired back against the gnarly bark, so aware of her nearness. "No. Story hour's not bothering me."

Eleanor pressed her lips together. Resting her head back against the trunk so near his own head, she sighed. "Okay. Forget I asked. I don't like it when people pry into my business—"

"My brothers and I want to give my parents a fortieth wedding anniversary party August 23. And we can't find a place to hold it. Everywhere we ask—the public parks and such—have been booked for a year in advance." He resisted the urge to reach toward her soft cheek.

"Why not ask at your church?" She glanced his way.

The glossy green leaves overhead whispered with the breeze, whispered, *Take her hand.* He ignored this. "We don't want to hold it at the church. You see, our church always holds a big shindig when a couple celebrates their fiftieth. My brothers and I don't want to wait that long—another ten years—and we want it to be held at a different place than the church. We want it to be different, special—from us to them. And a surprise, too, if we can pull it off," he said, as if he needed to explain anything to this astute woman.

"That makes sense. How many people are you expecting?" She looked to him.

Her immediate desire to help was so Eleanor. But Pete made a sound of amusement, a kind of snort. "There are a lot of Becks in Oneida

County. We want them all to come. And then a ton of friends, too."

"Ballpark figure?"

"Around one hundred and fifty." He resisted the urge to smooth a stray hair back from her face.

"Whew! That's a big order."

"I know. And I'm the oldest, and this party was my idea. And I can't seem to get it off the ground." He bent over and rested his elbows on his knees and bowed his head. Sitting down had unleashed more fatigue, fatigue due to distraction and worry. Maybe that was why Eleanor's attraction was affecting him so. "I'm bushed."

He felt her hand on his shoulder; he stopped breathing. The contact started a soothing warmth that spread from her touch through his back. He sighed aloud, letting it ripple through him. He silently begged her not to lift her hand. When she finally did, he leaned back. And found her nose a mere inch or so from his.

Her skin, though very fair, glowed with a subtle gold. Her green eyes gazed unabashedly into his. Her lips, a pale pink, beckoned him. He inhaled deeply and moved a fraction closer…closer. His lips brushed hers.

At the contact, she jerked backward as if stung.

Pete flushed with embarrassment. He rose

and cleared his throat. "I'm sorry I bothered you with my problem. I've got to go to Mike's shop. He wanted me to stop by before I went home."

"Okay," she said. "Bye."

Shock energized Pete. He gathered up his tools and headed for his pickup, not looking back. *I just kissed Eleanor Washburn. What was I thinking?*

I wasn't thinking, he concluded as he drove up to his brother's auto repair garage. *But I better be thinking and on my guard from now on. Sheesh, how will I be able to face her again?*

Hoping Mike had located a venue for the party, Pete walked into the garage bay area where he usually found his brother working underneath some car raised above him on the hoist. But today, he found it empty. Inhaling the combined aromas of gasoline and motor oil, he heard a peculiar noise coming from the back area where Mike stored parts and some cars he wanted to overhaul.

Pete walked into the room and waves hit him, rolled over him, one after the other. Not waves of water but sound waves. Though the noise wasn't at a dangerous level, instinctively he put his hands over his ears. Ahead of him, Mike stood beside a jazzed-up car. He wore protective earphones.

Hands still over his ears, Pete walked toward his brother. The closer he came to the car, the more the air around him vibrated. His work jeans started moving as if a deranged wind were blowing against his legs. *Mike must be out of his cotton-picking mind.* Pete nudged Mike with his elbow.

Mike swung around, and then he tapped the window. The sound waves stopped. Danny Miller, with his long, white-blond hair pulled back into a low ponytail, opened the car door; he, too, wore sound protection earphones.

"Hey, Pete," Mike said with a big grin and a smear of motor oil on his chin. "How'd you like that sound?"

Pete lowered his hands. "Are you out of your mind?" he asked, half joking, half serious.

"We got a real chance to win the db Drag Racing World Championship," Danny spoke up. "These new speakers are amazing. They can handle 162 decibels. We're entering the Super Street category."

"I repeat—are you two out of your minds?" Pete grinned, shaking his head at them.

"You college guys just don't get the seduction of sound—" Mike began.

From the front of the garage, a voice called out, "Hi! Where is everybody?"

The voice belonged to Eleanor. Remembering the near-kiss, Pete's face blazed. Unable to stop his reaction, he turned away from Mike to hide it. And even though he wanted to run the other way, he hurried to open the door. "Hi, we're in here."

She smiled and headed toward him. "You said you were going to be here and I wanted—"

"Hey!" Mike shouldered past Pete. "Glad to see you, Eleanor. Sorry I couldn't come and volunteer today. I'll try to come next Saturday afternoon."

Pete fell behind her, trying to cool his jets. He didn't want Eleanor here. He didn't want to see her now so soon after... The phantom touch of her lips on his rippled through him.

Eleanor offered Mike her hand. "I understand. I really have to juggle the hours at my practice during these Habitat projects."

Mike wiped his hand on a rag from his pocket and then shook hers. "Have you ever seen my place up close?"

"No, I always have my service done at the dealer. But you have an excellent reputation for good service."

"Nice to hear. Nice to hear." Mike beamed at her.

Was his brother trying to *start* something with Eleanor? Heat exploded inside Pete's gut. "Did I forget something at the site, Eleanor?" He shouldered past Mike to stand in front of Eleanor.

"No, no." She gazed at him, blushing slightly.

And he knew why. She must be remembering their almost-kiss just like he was. He wrapped his self-control even more tightly around himself. "Then?"

"I thought of a few places where you might hold your parents' party," she said.

Mike thumped Pete on the back. "I thought this was supposed to be all hush-hush."

"Oh, don't be upset with Pete," Eleanor hurried to say. "I kind of wheedled it out of him."

Pete did not recall any wheedling, but he let this pass. His emotions still wouldn't settle down. He forced himself to speak calmly. "You thought of someplace that could hold us?"

"Well, it's out of the way from here, but I thought of that big resort hotel in the Lakeland area. They let people hold weddings on their grounds. It's a bit of a drive, but the setting is lovely—on a lake in the forest, with a rustic but stately, whole-log-construction lodge in the background." She shrugged as if asking for opinions.

"Wow, that would be great," Mike said.

"Really cool," Danny Miller, standing just behind Mike, said.

"Oh, hello, Danny," Eleanor said, waving.

Pete fumed. Danny looked just as infatuated with Eleanor as Mike. Pete claimed Eleanor's arm. "Let's go into Mike's office and find the resort's phone number."

"Hey, Ms. Washburn," Danny said. "Want to see something cool?"

Mike chuckled. "Don't you mean *hear* something cool?"

Pete's irritation burned brighter. Mike's fascination with ear-shattering sound embarrassed Pete. But what could he say?

With one eyebrow raised, Eleanor looked to each one of them in turn. "Okay, I'll bite. What do you want me to hear?"

"After my experience," Pete said sourly, "I think Mike means *feel* rather than *hear*."

"Now you've got me going." Eleanor chuckled. "Show me."

Danny and Mike shepherded her to the rear of the room. Pete trailed after them, listening to Danny and Mike explain that they were going to Canada soon to compete in the db Drag Racing World Championship in car speakers. Then, with ear protection on, Danny climbed into the car, slammed the door. Mike handed both Pete and Eleanor earphones. And then it began.

Eleanor's eyes opened wide. She turned to Pete and mouthed, "Goodness." She pointed down to her flared jeans. They were vibrating, just as his slacks were.

Mike rapped on the window. The sound waves ceased. He tore off his earphones. "What do you think about that?"

Eleanor lifted off her own. "Amazing. I could feel the sound waves. Is it safe?"

"If we protect our ears," Mike said.

Danny climbed out of the car. "Isn't it crazy?"

Eleanor laughed. "I couldn't have said it better myself. Thanks, you two. I won't forget that very soon." She turned to leave, then halted. "Oh, Danny, you're not supposed to leave the county till—"

"It's not till late August," Danny said. "I'm hoping all my problems will be done by then."

"Okay." Eleanor headed to the door. "Which way is the office?"

Pete hurried after her. "I'll show you. Then Mike and Danny can go on with their testing."

Inside the neat but oil-tainted office, Pete pulled out the well-thumbed phone book. With Eleanor at his elbow inspecting a poster for synthetic motor oil, he called the number. He couldn't believe how smoothly the conversation went. When he hung up, he couldn't stop himself. He pulled Eleanor close for a quick hug.

He forced himself to release her. "Thank you!"

"Did they have room for you?" she asked.

"The weekend before the date. They had a wedding cancel. We'll have a tent and tables and chairs. And it's reasonable, too." He nearly hugged her again. But restrained himself.

Then Pete realized that Mike had entered during Pete's hug. Mike stared at him, freezing the spark in the pit of Pete's stomach. *Whoa.*

"Does all this hugging mean that Eleanor's idea panned out?" Mike asked gruffly.

"Yeah," Pete replied. "They have an opening on the Saturday before our parents' anniversary date. But we need to get on it right away."

"Well, it's Friday night," Mike said. "How about I take you up there for Fish Fry, Eleanor? And we'll look it over and see what we think. I don't like taking something sight unseen."

Pete pressed his lips together to hold back an objection to this plan. Of course, even a classy resort would observe the Wisconsin restaurant tradition of every Friday being Fish Fry night.

"Well—" Eleanor began.

The phone shrilled.

Mike picked up. "Mike's Garage and Tow." He made a face as he jotted something down.

He hung up. "I'll have to bow out, Eleanor. A good customer's car has stalled, and I need to head over there and see what's wrong."

"That's okay," Pete said. "I'll drive Eleanor up, and I'll take some photos of the place and get the scoop. How about that, Eleanor? Free for Fish Fry tonight?"

She glanced back and forth between them and then said, "Why not? I didn't have any plans." She looked down at her clothing. "The only thing is I don't want to eat there. I'm a little too dusty for that resort restaurant." She brushed a bit of sawdust from her sleeve.

"No problem. I know a great little out-of-the-way place. We'll stop at the resort and then head over there."

As he left the office, Mike shut the door a bit harder than needed.

Pete ignored him. "Let's take my truck." He knew he shouldn't have invited Eleanor; he knew he was playing with proverbial fire; but most of all he knew he couldn't stop himself.

After they left Eleanor's car in her garage, the drive to the resort proved to be a silent one. The almost-kiss at the Habitat site inhibited Eleanor. No man had kissed her for over two years. Probably that explained why it had affected her so. But could she break the awkward silence here and now? She didn't relish a whole evening of this. And how to let Pete know she wasn't mad at him for kissing her, but that she and Pete could only be friends?

She decided to jump in and start a conversation, hoping it would lead to a point where she could make this all clear to him. "It's really great that you want to honor your parents."

Pete nodded, his eyes on the road.

"It's rare nowadays that anybody stays married." As soon as the words left her mouth, she cringed. Not the right thing to say to a man who had lost his wife.

"You got that right."

She analyzed Pete's tone. Definitely bitter. Should she change the subject?

"Sorry. I'm not being very good company," Pete said, glancing her way.

"It's Friday and it's been a busy week," she said mildly.

He almost chuckled. "You're being kind. But I'm at fault for my own hard feelings. My breakup was messy. And it kind of spills over sometimes onto other things. Other people."

Eleanor drew in the warm summer air blowing in the windows. "I've not been lucky in love, either. And people are always trying to set me up. They mean well. But..."

"But no one can choose someone for us," Pete said, glancing sideways at her.

"Exactly. Being single in a couples' world…" She shrugged.

"Yeah, it's hard. Two of my brothers are married and happy."

"More pressure?" she asked.

"Yeah."

Eleanor eased inside. This conversation had cleared the air some. Being alone was hard, but not as hard as being alone while *in* a relationship. Neither of her fiancés were interested in her as a person. That had happened to her twice. *And it won't happen a third time.* "My Aunt Mavis made a life for herself without being married. And not surprisingly, she usually doesn't meddle with matchmaking."

"Maybe she can have a good influence on my mom." He grinned teasingly. "My mom's great, but she wants to see me happily married. However, second marriages are harder to do right than first ones. I can't take chances with my kids."

"I agree completely." Her attraction to Pete stirred now. Remembering the touch of his lips made her tingle with the memory.

"You do?"

"Yes. Pete, I really like Cassie and love being with her, but I'm not trying to use her to get to you." Eleanor was surprised to hear these words come out. Should she bring up the kiss?

"Now that's honesty."

They were arriving at the outskirts of Island City. Tall evergreen trees surrounded the lodge which faced the highway. Pete drove in and parked by the imposing entrance.

Before he got out, he said, "Thanks for saying that. I want you and Cassie to be friends. I just didn't want her to get hurt, you know, start thinking of some woman as more than a friend. Does that make sense?"

"Exactly. But I know how much Aunt Mavis added to my life. If Cassie forms a friendship with me, I won't let her down. Promise." As she said this, she thought again of her plans to adopt a child. Should she share these with Pete? She pushed this aside—along with the memory of the touch of his lips on hers.

"Great." He got out and met her at the front of the truck. Soon the events manager, a young woman in denim and a resort T-shirt, was showing them the grounds and discussing options and costs for Pete's parents' anniversary party. Pete clicked several photos with his cell phone.

Eleanor followed, just listening. The two-story resort restaurant, situated in the rear, overlooked the lake, and its lower level opened onto a terrace where a few tables sat. She heard the laughter and chatter of many voices, cheery sounds. Then she heard, "Eleanor! Eleanor, is that you?"

She froze where she stood. It couldn't be.

"Eleanor!" A tall man turned her, hugged her and then kissed her on the cheek.

She pulled herself away. "Rick, hi." She hoped her less-than-welcoming tone would discourage him.

"Great to see you!" Rick boomed, turning more heads from the terrace and deck above toward them. "I was just thinking about you yesterday!"

Unfortunately her former fiancé was still as good-looking as ever. However, seeing him stirred nothing but the need to distance herself from him.

Then to Eleanor's horror, he picked her up for an extended bear hug.

"Hi," Pete said loudly at Eleanor's side. "I'm Pete. Evidently you know Eleanor."

Rick lowered her to the ground. She stumbled, and Pete pulled her to him and put an obviously possessive arm around her. Her senses reeled; her face burned.

"Oh, hi. I'm Rick. Eleanor and I were involved once. Just saying hi." Rick's slight slurring of his words told Eleanor the man had already had one or two too many drinks. Another reason she'd broken off with this "charming" real estate agent.

Pete offered his hand. "Rick, nice to meet you."

"Come on in, and I'll buy you two a drink." Rick shook hands and then repeated his invitation with a wave toward the restaurant and bar.

"Thanks," Pete said. "But we'll pass. We have reservations somewhere else."

Eleanor could have kissed Pete right then and there.

"Good. Good." The collar of Rick's light yellow sports shirt was open, and he was dressed in his customary crisp khakis. "Glad to see Eleanor's found someone else. Our breakup was sad. But I couldn't go through with our engagement when I knew it wasn't best for both of us."

If she hadn't been struck dumb by the situation, Eleanor would have been glad to set the record straight. *I ended our engagement, Rick. You didn't. But of course everything was always all about you.*

"Nice meeting you." Pete drew Eleanor away with him. And she was grateful. The embarrassing heat drained from her face, and her breathing returned to normal again. No woman would be embarrassed to be on Pete's arm.

Inside a small office, Pete signed a few papers and handed the events manager a check to reserve the date for the party. Then he and Eleanor headed to his truck.

Soon he was driving them down a county road to the small, out-of-the-way place he'd mention earlier. She wished she could say something, but she couldn't. Rick had vacated her life completely and had left only a lingering distaste. Why had he come up to her tonight?

"I missed Fish Fry night when I lived in Las Vegas," Pete said.

Recognizing Pete's gambit to get them back to normal, Eleanor turned to look squarely at him. "Las Vegas?"

"That's where I went to school. And got married...and divorced."

Was he trying to take the sting out of her meeting Rick? She gave him a half smile for trying. But meeting Rick had underlined and put into bold lettering why she needed to keep her distance from Pete, even now, after their earlier reassuring conversation.

"I know this is a cliché, but can we just be friends?" Pete glanced her way. "I'm not looking for more than that now."

"Yes," Eleanor interrupted him. "Yes, we can be friends. Romance is just too...chancy. We both have busy lives. And I'm not ready to embark on a new romance right now. Does that make sense?"

"Yeah, it does," he agreed in a wry tone. He left the county road for a narrower road that began to wind around a little, sky-blue lake, sparkling through the trees. "So, tell me about your week. Do you have any interesting cases you can talk about?"

Thank you, Pete. She drew in a deep breath, leaned back in her seat and began to talk about a client who had jumped bail. She relished his attention and intelligent comments. And didn't think of kissing him again—okay, only once. This attraction would pass, but their friendship wouldn't have to—if she stuck to her anti-romance guns.

Pete turned down one winding road after another through a forest of evergreens. Here and there, the hint of a cabin or cottage or lake could be glimpsed through the trees, but mostly forest surrounded them. Finally they came to the entrance of the small resort, Hidden Lake. He drove into a parking spot.

She got out of the truck, smiling. The unpretentious resort, a long, low log house, surrounded by small log cabins nestled within the pines, charmed her. Pete put his name in with the hostess and then led Eleanor out to walk near the lake while they waited for a table.

"Lake's high," he said.

"Lots of snow and then lots of rain," she replied, admiring his profile.

He picked up a rock and threw it so it skipped across the top of the water.

Eleanor sat down on a lakeside bench. "Tell me what you have planned for your parents' anniversary party."

He settled down beside her. "Not much. We were kind of holding off on specific details until we found a place to throw the party."

"Hey!" A loud voice boomed behind them. "I thought I'd find you here."

Startled, Eleanor turned to see Mike striding toward them. "I thought you had to help that customer."

"Yeah, I did that, and then I got a AAA call to tow someone just outside Island City. When I finished, I thought I'd take a chance and see if you two were here. I know this is Pete's favorite restaurant up here."

Eleanor looked at the faces of the two brothers, and they didn't look happy with each other. But she was relieved. Now this didn't feel like a date at all, and she could relax. Or could she? Pete's expression was becoming more and more stormy. Did he see his brother as competition? Why? Hadn't Pete stated that he wasn't interested in dating? *Men. Who could understand them?*

Chapter Six

The threesome broke up after dinner, and Pete now drove up to Eleanor's neat house with detached garage. He approved of her choice of home. She'd bought one of those solidly built, sixties ranches. He admired the stonework around the lower half of the exterior. He cut the engine and sat back. The twilight sunshine lingered around them, golden, nearly thick enough to touch. He didn't know what to think about Mike dropping in on them at Hidden Lake. What had Eleanor thought of that?

Usually Mike's and his tastes in women didn't coincide. *Why am I thinking that? Since Suzann left me, I've been distancing myself from women, especially young, single women. But it's normal for me to notice a beautiful woman. However, I can't mislead a woman, especially this woman.* His thoughts chased themselves around in his mind. How could he sort this all out?

Eleanor cleared her throat. "You and I already discussed that I'm not interested in having a relationship right now after two failed engagements. And maybe never, with my track record.... I mean—you met Rick." Eleanor fell silent, her soft mouth twisting into an unhappy line.

Relationship? Why was she bringing this up again? Was it because of Mike barging in this evening? And making it look like they were jockeying for her attention? Since he didn't know what to say, he made a sound of nominal agreement.

She had lowered her chin, and he had to resist the urge to lift it, if only to enjoy gazing at her. He didn't like to see her downcast like this. "What is it?" he murmured.

Her head came up, but she didn't turn toward him. "There is another particular reason that I can't give time to a relationship right now."

Pete considered asking her what this reason could be. But should he become more involved in this woman's life, even as a friend? Then he recalled the courtroom scene and Danny Miller's mother's confidences about how kind Eleanor had been to her. Yes, he wanted to know why a good person like Eleanor was as anti-relationship as he. Finally, he asked cautiously, "Do you want to share what that is?"

She slid her back against the pickup door, facing him. The evening breeze wafted in, stirring her hair. The twilight sun made her hair shine with gold highlights. "I haven't told anybody other than Mavis so far. But I plan on adopting a child from the foster care system."

Of all the things he might have expected her to say, this wasn't it. Though he really had no idea what he had expected her to reveal. However, this triggered a memory, one that sent a wave of sharp pain through him.

"Biological clock ticking?" he muttered archly, mimicking his ex-wife's stated reason for wanting to start their family. The family she had rejected so swiftly, so easily when she found motherhood demanded more than she wanted to give. A sharply painful memory flashed within—his wife folding a pillow around her ears to block the sound of Nicky screaming with colic.

"Probably." She shrugged. "Do you think I'm crazy?"

Pete closed his mouth, sorting through the blasts of his own suffering and regret that ricocheted through him. *This is Eleanor, not Suzann.* "No, I don't think you're crazy."

"I don't think I'm going to marry." She gave

a wry smile, answering his next question. "At least not in the near future. I want to be a mother, love a child who needs love."

Her tender tone and sincere words touched Pete more deeply than he would have expected. Giving into impulse, he took her hand. "You'll be a great mom."

Tears sprang to Eleanor's eyes. She looked away, no doubt to hide them. But she didn't withdraw her hand from his. "Thank you."

"Have you begun the process of adoption yet?" he asked.

She turned back to him and smiled, her whole face lighting up. "Yes, I have an interview this week. For now this has to be my focus in my personal life."

"Great." He squeezed her hand and then withdrew his, resisting the tempting urge to pull her closer. He breathed easier. "I hope you'll keep me posted. And you can be Cassie's friend. I was being overly cautious."

Her smile broadened. "I can't deny that her choosing me to be her special friend gave me extra confidence to proceed with this. I've never been around children much. I was an only child, and so were both of my parents, so I don't even have cousins."

"Wow," he muttered.

She chuckled. "I know you have a huge family. I found that out when I looked for your number and saw all the Becks in the phone book."

He chuckled then. "Yeah, we're a prolific bunch and have stayed tied to the land. Our ancestor, who is my namesake, Peter Beck, arrived from Baden-Baden, Germany, in 1846, and he bought the land that my dad still farms."

"Wow," she said. "That's unusual."

"I broke free for a time. Went to school in Las Vegas and then settled there." He stopped then, not wanting to go into why he'd come home with his tail between his legs and two little babies in his arms. He swallowed that down once more.

"I was born and raised in Madison and never strayed far. My parents taught at University of Wisconsin there," Eleanor said, opening her purse and pulling out her keys. "Now I owe you a Fish Fry sometime. Don't forget."

He didn't like her mentioning this. "What's a Fish Fry between friends?" he asked.

She laughed at this, opened her door, and left with a friendly, "Good night!" and a wave.

He watched till she got inside and then he turned backed down the driveway. This evening had given him a lot to think about—Mike's interest in Eleanor and his own clinging to the past. Time to break free. He still couldn't believe that Eleanor had ever been engaged to a big bag of wind like Rick. *Sheesh*.

After last night's Fish Fry threesome, Pete eyed Mike with misgiving the next afternoon, Saturday, at the Habitat site. Clouds scudded overhead, heralding another storm front approaching faster than predicted. Humidity had zoomed. The sound of hammers and nail guns punctuated the hum of voices.

Kevan arrived with another man with the same build as Kevan but with salt and pepper hair and a lined face. "Hey, Pete!" Kevan called out, "Come meet my uncle Dex!"

Pete shook the man's hand. "Hi, Dex, glad you could come."

"My pleasure," Dex replied with a friendly grin. "I know which end of a hammer to hold. What's there for me to do?"

Pete led them over to a group that was framing walls.

After noon, Mike had closed his shop for the weekend, arrived and gravitated to Pete. Now they were laying the subfloor. Mike did not look happy; Pete did not feel happy. Pete was the eldest and Mike the next son, so they had been rivals as children. But never before as adults. And never over a woman. *That's why this feels so odd.*

*How can I say I'm not trying to start some-
thing with Eleanor? And furthermore that
she isn't interested in starting anything with
anyone?* How could he get that across to Mike
without sounding…conceited. How to put this
situation into words baffled Pete.

Fortunately, navigating the floor joists, carrying subflooring didn't give them a chance
to talk much. Finally, they both stopped for a
drink of water from a large, plastic cooler and
sat on the grass under a tree.

"So you took Eleanor home last night?" Mike
muttered, wiping his brow with his sleeve.

Pete wondered how he should respond and
decided to be frank. "I'm not trying to start
something with her."

Mike humphed.

"I'm not." Pete decided to go further. "And
we had an embarrassing moment at the resort."

"Oh?"

"Ran into a guy she'd been engaged to once."

"Ouch." Mike crinkled up his face.

"I think she's been burned bad."

Mike glanced at Pete. "You think she's
gun-shy?"

Pete nodded. "Seriously."

"I don't think we'd really be a good match,
but she's a woman no man should take lightly."

Mike's words struck Pete as absolutely true.

The conversation halted there because Eleanor approached them. "Hi, Mike."

"Hey," Mike replied, rising.

Pete stood and studied her face. Something was worrying her, and he didn't like that.

"Can either of you think of a way to keep this project moving?"

"What do you mean?" Pete asked.

Her mouth drew down into a deep frown. "Rain is predicted every day starting tomorrow. We need to get the roof up, but it's not possible if we can't stay dry long enough to get the ceiling joists and the roof sheeting up."

A raindrop plunked on Pete's nose.

All three of them looked up and groaned in unison.

Eleanor turned and shouted, "Get the tarps! Rain!"

Rain pelted down as the volunteers quickly covered all the materials and the shell of a house with heavy plastic tarps. Pete hurried to do his part, and a germ of an idea came to him. But he'd have to find out if it would work and see if he could get permission. He wanted to keep this project moving, but most of all, he wanted to make life easier for Eleanor.

Eleanor wished her stomach would stop swirling like a washing machine on Agitate.

Why did everything have to be perfect today? *My parents and Mavis are coming for lunch. What's the big deal?* The big deal was today she wanted to persuade her parents that she was just as capable at home as in the courtroom. And this would be their first visit since they'd retired to Arizona and the first time they visited her in this house.

But of course, her nerves jumped today because she might tell them about her adoption plans. *Dear Lord, help me focus. Or at least breathe.*

Buzzing with tension, she bustled around her kitchen, recipes spread out on the counter. Whole wheat rotini bubbled on the stove top, as did eggs. Her menu included all her parents' favorite summer foods: deviled eggs, cantaloupe and pasta salad with chickpeas. Chicken breasts were marinating in the fridge to be grilled later.

A vigorous rapping sounded on her back door. She glanced at the clock. Her guests were early. "Come in!" she called out, shoving down her nervousness. Or trying to.

Pete walked in the back door. "Eleanor!"

She nearly dropped the spoon she was stirring in the boiling rotini. "Pete?"

"I got a great idea—"

The sound of car doors slamming outside interrupted him. The back door opened.

"Eleanor!" her father, John, called out.

"Dad!" Eleanor set down the spoon, gave Pete an apologetic smile and hurried to the back door.

Her father's long legs made short work of the back hall. He embraced her. "Eleanor!"

She wrapped her arms around her silver-haired dad and breathed in the scent of Old Spice aftershave, the fragrance that always meant "Dad."

Her tall, long-limbed mother, Delia, who wore her thick salt-and-pepper hair pulled back severely into a long tail, appeared behind him. "Eleanor," she said in that controlled way of hers.

Eleanor stepped back from her father and accepted the hand her mother offered. "Mother."

"You're looking well," Delia said, not looking at Eleanor but at Pete through her gold-rimmed glasses.

"Sorry, I didn't know you were having family over today," Pete said, edging toward the doorway now blocked by her mother.

"Don't run off," John said, offering his hand to Pete. "I'm John, Eleanor's dad."

Pete shook John's hand.

"I'm Delia," her mother said, merely nodding and then pressing her lips together.

Suddenly Eleanor bristled. Pete had every right to drop in. Why did her mother always "freeze" any man she thought Eleanor might be interested in? *You married, Mother. Why am I supposed to be Ms. Super-Feminist Career Woman and stay single?* "This is Pete Beck," Eleanor said, making the introductions as smoothly as silk.

Though she didn't want a man in her life right now, she wouldn't let her mother think she couldn't have one if she wanted one. "Pete's the building-trades teacher at the local high school, and he's one of my main volunteers at the final Habitat site."

"Great," John said, smiling. He moved to the counter and leaned against it. "Teaching young men—"

"And young women, I hope," Delia interrupted tartly.

"—and young women," John added agreeably, "to work with their hands must be very satisfying."

"I like it. It's a challenge." Pete looked quizzically at Delia, who was still studying him with a frown. "And I did have two female students this last year. Power tools make a big difference. There are some jobs that are harder for females, and some easier. They can fit in tight places better than most guys."

Eleanor could have kissed Pete for his common sense reply. Her mother's feminism often reached the grating level.

"And our Eleanor has certainly proven that a woman can get a house built," Delia said briskly. "Two in a year, in fact."

At this uncommon compliment from her mother, shock and pleasure vied within Eleanor.

"Yeah, Eleanor keeps us all moving, and we need to," Pete agreed. "However, we've had a rainy summer so far. That's delayed us."

Eleanor turned to the stove to check on her pasta.

"Eleanor, that's why I came today," Pete continued. "I called the school—"

Another car door slammed and the back door opened. "It's me, Mavis! Sorry I'm late!" Mavis joined the kitchen gathering.

Eleanor had a small kitchen but now it had become standing room only. "Hi, Auntie."

"Pete?" Mavis said. "Didn't expect to see you here."

"I didn't mean to intrude on a family gathering," Pete said. "But this saves me calling you, Mavis. I have time this week to come over and inspect your house. Which afternoon is best for you?"

"Any afternoon except Monday. Your mom is taking us to a flea market farther north. Some town…" Mavis paused, obviously trying to recall the name.

Eleanor caught her mother looking at Pete's hand. For a wedding band? Or a white line where one had been? Eleanor steamed.

"St. Germain," Pete supplied. "Mom loves that flea market. Every Monday." Pete turned to Eleanor. "I'll call you later," he murmured.

The roar of a motorcycle interrupted him, sounding loud and near.

All their heads swung toward the driveway-side window.

"Hey!" Mike roared as he opened the back door. "Is that Pete's pickup parked at the curb?" Mike filled the doorway, and the small kitchen seemed to shrink further.

"Hi, Mike!" Eleanor called out over the crowd between them. "I thought I recognized that Harley engine."

"Hey, Eleanor! You got a crowd here." Mike leaned against the doorjamb of the back hall.

"Why don't we seniors," Mavis said, gesturing toward the doorway, "move into the living room or outside?"

Now her mother was scrutinizing Mike, and Eleanor nearly chuckled. Mike, with his Harley

T-shirt and leather wristbands, didn't apologize for who he was. Eleanor liked that about him.

The stove timer dinged. Turning her back to everyone, she lifted the large pot off the stove. She set the pot on a trivet and sampled the pasta. *"Al dente."* She quickly poured the noodles and boiled eggs into the colander in the sink, hoping when she looked up the kitchen would have cleared out.

It hadn't.

"What can I do for you, Mike?" Eleanor asked brightly.

"Nothin' special. Just saw Pete's pickup here and wanted to ask him something." Mike waved a large hand toward his brother.

"Excuse me." Pete hurried past Mavis to his brother. The two of them went outside.

Eleanor realized both her parents were staring at her. She looked at Mavis, who just chuckled. Eleanor needed some space to breathe. She asked, "Why don't you all just go out and find a comfortable chair—"

Another car door slammed outside.

Eleanor began to feel a bit dazed. Usually her little house sat silent with only her own footsteps sounding on the hardwood floors.

The back door opened. "Hello!"

Eleanor recognized Kevan Paxton's voice. "Come in, Kevan!"

But Jenelle with Tiesha in hand appeared first. "So sorry to drop in on you. I didn't realize that you were entertaining."

"No problem," Eleanor said. She introduced Jenelle, Tiesha, Kevan and his Uncle Dex, who greeted everybody, although his gaze settled on Mavis.

"We won't stay. We're just showing Dex around our new hometown," Kevan said.

Eleanor wondered if Mavis was aware of the way Dex was looking at her. She must be, because she was trying not to look at Dex.

Then—unbelievably—another car door slammed somewhere outside. *Please, Lord, let it be at my neighbor's.* But she recognized the feminine voice outside.

Mavis grinned sheepishly.

The back door opened and little feet in flip-flops raced inside. "Miss Ellie! Miss Ellie!" Cassie ignored the other adults and went straight to Eleanor. The little girl held up her hands.

Naturally, Eleanor swung her up. "Cassie? What a nice surprise. Why are you here?" She grinned at Pete's daughter, her heart expanding.

"Grandma's got something for you." Cassie looked to Eleanor's father. "Hi." Cassie waved at him. "Hi."

"Hi yourself." John took her hand in his and

greeted her warmly. "You are a pretty little girl. Just like little Tiesha."

"Thank you!" Cassie crowed. Then she glimpsed her friend and squirmed down to run to her.

Pete's mother, Kerry Ann, strolled inside, wearing a pair of blue shorts and a green Hodag T-shirt. "Eleanor, I heard you were having your parents over for a cookout so I brought you some salad fixings from my garden." Kerry Ann held up an oak basket overflowing with leaf lettuce, fresh spinach, green onions and endive. "I even have a few early cherry tomatoes from my greenhouse."

"Mother, Dad," Eleanor said, "this is Pete and Mike's mom, Kerry Ann Beck, and this is Pete's daughter, Cassie." Everyone greeted each other.

Eleanor watched her mother's expression turn more and more speculative. Eleanor stiffened. Her friends had a right to drop by whenever, and she wouldn't apologize. But that didn't stop her stomach from knotting. Her mother only wanted her to associate with people *she* thought worthy. "Thanks so much. Would you like a tall iced tea?"

"Sounds wonderful. And I noticed you have a nice patio out back. Why are we all inside on this rare, sunny afternoon?" Kerry Ann gestured toward the door.

"We'll be going," Kevan said.

"No, stay for a while," Mavis said, motioning them to follow her outside. "I know Eleanor has plenty of iced tea and lemonade. I'm just getting to know people here."

Dex grinned. "Kevan has been trying to talk me into moving here, too. Says he wants some family close by."

"Well, I just moved here, and so far, I love this area," Mavis said, walking to the back hall.

John held out his arms to Cassie. "Want to go outside?"

"Cassie, do come outside," Kerry Ann called over her shoulder. "I brought bubbles."

"Oh!" Cassie launched herself at John. "Bubbles. Let's go blow bubbles. Can Tiesha blow some, too?"

John caught her. "Sounds like a plan." He led the girls outside, chuckling. The Paxtons followed.

Only her mother remained. "You seem to have a lot of friends here."

"Yes, I do." Eleanor wished her mother didn't make her feel taut and insecure.

Before her mother could say more, Pete and Mike re-entered. Pete cleared his throat. "Eleanor, I know you're busy, but Mike and I need you for just a minute." Her mother grimaced and left. Pete smiled in his way that melted Eleanor's resistance. "I think I know how we can avoid any further rain delays."

Eleanor moved toward him. How did he always manage to draw her nearer? "You did?"

"I checked with the principal and superintendent of the high school. They said I can borrow the big tent the school owns for community gatherings."

Mike spoke up, making both of them step back and turn toward him. "Guys, I hate to interrupt but I'm heading out. I was on my way to pick up a part at the auto supply. I'll see you two at the Habitat site if not sooner." He lifted a large hand and left, exchanging friendly goodbyes.

"Tent?" Eleanor returned to the topic. "You mean you'd put the tent up over the shell?"

"Exactly."

"Have you measured to see if it's big enough?"

He pulled a folded piece of paper from his jeans' pocket. "The Paxtons' house is a ranch so the tent will rise to about three feet above the peak of their roof and will actually cover the whole house and—"

"That's wonderful!" Her mood soared. Unable to stop herself, she threw her arms around him. "I've been trying and trying to come up with a way to move things along."

She knew she should release him but couldn't. His strength bolstered hers. "The house must be ready before Jenelle brings home their new baby in late August."

"Eleanor," her father called from the back door, "should I fire up the grill yet?"

Hearing his footsteps, she leapt back from Pete as if they'd been kissing or something, grateful her dad had come in, not her mother. Their recent near-kiss at the Habitat site flashed in her mind.

"Do you have enough chicken for our guests?" her dad asked.

"Yes, I think so." She took another step away from Pete.

Pete moved toward her dad and the back door. "I didn't come to party crash."

"Pete, I'm enjoying your daughter so much," John objected. "Why don't you stay for a while longer?"

Eleanor wondered why her dad had said this. Did he think she and Pete were involved? Her cheeks were flaming, a telltale sign.

"I don't want to intrude," Pete said, obviously hesitant.

"Hey, the Paxtons are making sounds of leaving. If you go, too, I'm the only guy here. Have a heart." John grinned.

Pete nodded, suddenly grinning, too. "Okay. If you've been blowing bubbles with Cassie, she won't be ready to leave yet."

Eleanor watched this male bonding, still struggling with her confusion over Pete.

"Why don't you go outside with my dad, Pete?" Eleanor turned to the sink, wanting time to compose herself before her mother saw her again.

"I think I'll stay in here for a moment," Pete said tentatively, "and help you get what you're going to whip up and then we'll go outside together."

Why did he want to stay? Suddenly, uneasiness grabbed the back of her neck.

Deserting them, John headed toward the door. "I'll light the charcoal, and you bring the chicken breasts out when you want me to get them started."

"Okay, Dad." Eleanor faced Pete and found him much closer than she'd expected. She couldn't be unhappy he was staying. His presence somehow strengthened her, in spite of her mother's unspoken disapproval.

"I like your dad," Pete said, only a few inches from her, his breath tickling her ear.

"I do, too," she murmured, his nearness igniting a glow from within. A swift clutch of coldness followed this warmth. *Mother will not be happy if Pete, Kerry Ann and Cassie stay.*

She'd always accepted her mother's extreme feminism as a fact of life. Now, and not for the first time, she wondered what could be the root of this hard bone of contention between them. Why did her mother want Eleanor to remain single? Eleanor had never come up with a cause.

When it came to Eleanor, her mother behaved like a surly watchdog, as if she had to guard her daughter from any sign of weakness or traditional femininity. *I'm not a weak, helpless female. I'm a successful professional woman. What is with my mother? I'm going to have to find out once and for all.*

Kevan stepped inside, refusing an invitation to stay. He left with a friendly wave.

Within very few minutes, Pete had helped Eleanor assemble the pasta salad. All the greens Kerry Ann had brought were freshly washed, and it took only moments for Eleanor to combine them into a large salad bowl. Then Pete helped scoop out the hard-boiled yolks for the deviled eggs.

"You better let me go outside now," Pete said teasingly. "I'm a fiend when it comes to deviled eggs. Not many will actually reach the table if I stay."

"Would you take the chicken breasts with you? They're in the fridge in a large, clear, Tupperware bowl."

"I can do that." Pete moved away, and she missed his presence immediately.

He whistled as he carried the large bowl outside. The sound lifted her spirits higher. *I will not let my mother ruin today. I'm happy Pete, Kerry Ann and Cassie have come. Why can't I have friends that aren't all college professors?*

It's my life after all. Eleanor set the plate of deviled eggs beside the pasta salad in the fridge. Then, removing her apron, she brought out her pitcher of fresh lemonade and her platter of appetizers. She lifted her chin and walked toward the door. *It's my party, and I'll have a good time if I want to.*

Chapter Seven

After the appetizers had been devoured, John and Pete used the instant thermometer to check the temperature of the chicken breasts and declared them ready to eat. All of them sat at Eleanor's new picnic table. Cassie insisted on sitting beside Eleanor. Cassie's preference for her still touched Eleanor deeply. Also by request, her dad sat on Cassie's other side.

"You have a charming daughter," her dad said to Pete.

"I have a son, too," Pete said. "He's with his grandfather today, riding the tractor."

"Is that safe?" Delia asked sharply.

"Quite safe," Kerry Ann said. "This is modern farming. My husband and Nicky are sitting in an air-conditioned cab."

John chuckled. "I've never been on a tractor.

Do you think your husband would let me ride along sometime this summer?"

"I'll ask him." Kerry Ann smiled and dug her fork into the greens she'd brought.

Eleanor tried to keep herself occupied with being a good hostess and ignoring her mother's intimidating and ominous silence. She had no luck with this, or with disregarding how Pete ignited her awareness of him—his every expression, intonation, movement. Too soon, the summer lunch had been eaten, and Kerry Ann, Cassie and Pete had risen to leave.

"It was nice to meet Eleanor's parents," Kerry Ann said, taking Cassie's hand. "I'll see you at home later, Pete."

"Yeah, I've got some errands to run," Pete said. "Eleanor, thanks again for lunch. I'll make arrangements to bring the tent out and get it set up. Then we can finish the shell and enclose everything—rain or shine."

Unable to stop herself, Eleanor went to him and took his hand, squeezing it. She tried not to show how he affected her. "Thanks, Pete. This is a great idea."

As Kerry Ann led Cassie away, the little girl turned and called, "Miss Ellie, will you come and swing with me again at my grandma's house?"

Eleanor grinned, hiding her deeper reaction.

How could anyone reject this sweet child? "I'll try. Bye, Cassie!" The three of them disappeared from sight. She turned back to her parents and Aunt Mavis. "I'll get busy and put the leftovers away. Then I'll come back out with more lemonade."

"I'm sorry," Delia said, abruptly rising from her lawn chair. "I have some emailing to do. I need to go to Mavis's."

"Delia," John objected. "Email can wait. We're spending the afternoon, the whole afternoon, with our daughter as planned."

"The guests have left—"

Her mother's dismissal of her lit the fire. Eleanor burst into invisible flames. "We have something to discuss, something important."

Delia swung her attention to Eleanor, looking worried.

"I'm adopting a child." Eleanor said the words as a challenge.

Mavis shook her head at Eleanor as if scolding her for lack of finesse.

Both Eleanor's parents gawked at her. Her father recovered first. "That's a big decision. Do you mean a child or an infant?"

Eleanor sank into the nearest lawn chair, suddenly deflated. "I've already spoken to a social worker about adopting a child from the foster care system. There are a few little girls whose parental rights have been severed."

Delia remained silent, her mouth slammed shut.

How long would that last? Eleanor wondered.

"I take it you've given this a lot of thought?" John asked, obviously choosing each word with care.

"Yes. Of course I have." Eleanor brushed back wisps of hair disturbed by the warm breeze. "I want to be a mother, but I don't seem to connect with the kind of man I'd like to marry. And I'll be thirty-three this December. It's time to do this."

"I'm happy," Mavis said, "that Eleanor cares enough about others to want to give a child a home and a mother."

Delia threw her hands upward. "Why would you want to tie yourself down with a child? You're young. You should be traveling, care-free."

"I know you never let yourself be tied down with a child," Eleanor said. The words spoken low grated in her throat. "Aunt Mavis raised—"

"I loved my career," Delia interrupted. "You should be thankful that I did. I tried to help you grow up to be independent, self-sufficient."

"Eleanor is a successful woman with a career," her father said soothingly. "Why can't she adopt a child if she wants to?"

Delia turned brusquely. "She can do whatever she wants. I really must go now. While I'm here, the archeological dig in Utah needs me to keep in touch with them."

Eleanor rose and blocked her mother's exit. "Mother, I want your support. This little girl will become your granddaughter." *And I won't have her slighted by you.*

"Eleanor, I'm not the kind of woman who can't be happy *without* grandchildren."

"That's not the issue. This isn't about you, Mother. It's about the child I'll adopt. Will you welcome her into the family?"

"Of course." Delia moved around her. "Just don't expect me to don an apron and have her over to bake cookies." She glanced toward her husband. "Mavis can bring you home with her. I'll be in the office at Mavis's." With a quick thank-you, Delia hurried down the drive and disappeared around the house.

"Why is she like that?" Eleanor asked, sitting down, feeling abandoned.

Neither John nor Mavis replied for a few beats. Then her father came over and sat in the chair next to hers and took her hand. "Your mother loves you. You have to believe that. But there is a reason why she is as she is."

"What is the reason?"

"That is something that you and your mother need to thrash out together." Her father rose and gathered bowls of leftover food and headed for the kitchen.

Eleanor looked across at Mavis.

"Honey, your mother loves you. And this is something that you should have confronted her about long ago."

"How could I?" Eleanor asked sarcastically. "She was never around me long enough for a deep discussion."

And Eleanor knew that she'd avoided deep discussions with her mother, too. Their connection had been too tenuous, too insecure to test with honesty. She'd always hoped that someday she would have done enough to win her mother's affection. And with that reassurance, she could have discussed the things that mattered most.

Mavis rose. "Come, let's clean up. You need to pray about this."

Eleanor, feeling wearier than she should, rose and obeyed. "Will you pray about it, Auntie?"

Mavis squeezed Eleanor's shoulder. "Honey, I've been praying about this for years."

Under an overcast sky, Pete drove up New Friends Street and parked in front of the Habitat site, ready to get the tent up so the project could catch up with the planned building schedule. Eleanor already stood near the lonely-looking, roofless shell. A few volunteers, including Dex, Kevan's uncle, who'd come to help put up the tent, milled around in the unusually heavy humidity. Pete called to them. Soon the six of them were carrying the rolled-up canvas tent.

With Eleanor directly across from him, Pete couldn't stop himself from glancing at her with concern. Ever since sharing lunch with her and her family a few days ago, he'd turned the troubling impressions of her family over and over in his mind. His family had stresses. Didn't every family? But Eleanor's mother had seemed to him… What? He didn't know what to call it, other than not happy. Should he say something or remain silent?

Eleanor had helped him with his problem, and he wanted to help her. Didn't friends help friends? And wasn't that what he was doing today? Pete preferred dealing with real stuff, wood and nails, not all that touchy-feely stuff.

Right now, he had to stop thinking about Eleanor and her family and start getting this tent up. First the six of them unrolled it, and then using ladders, he and another volunteer hefted it over the roof. While they were working on the supports and stakes, he managed to stand next to Eleanor. He murmured into her ear, "I'm going to Mavis's soon to inspect her house."

"I'm glad you're going to make sure it's ready for winter," she said.

He nodded, unable to look away. The delicate curve of her ear had captured his gaze. "I like her, and I like her house. It was built solidly, but every house needs maintenance."

She made that humming agreement sound, but her mind definitely appeared to have drifted off to something else. But what?

Eleanor had hurried home from the Habitat site before the social worker, Ms. Green, arrived. *I hope I let Pete know how much I appreciated his getting that tent.* But if she hadn't, she'd make up for it.

She walked through her house, making sure not a speck of dust remained. Though she tried, she couldn't get her low mood to budge. Her mother's dark presence seemed to hang over her, sucking out her bright hope to adopt Jenna, the little girl in the photo Ms. Green had showed her. Would this adoption separate Eleanor ever further from her mother?

Eleanor was just wiping down the gleaming kitchen counter one more time when the doorbell rang. Her heart bobbed up into her throat.

She opened the door and Ms. Green, dressed in khakis and a crisp blouse, greeted her.

Eleanor stepped back to let her in and tried not to show her agitation.

"There's no need for you to be nervous," Ms. Green said.

"Guess my nonchalant mask isn't working." Chuckling with the woman helped ease Eleanor's tension. Still, her mother's unhappy expression kept bobbing up, cinching a tight band around Eleanor's lungs.

"Why don't you show me around first?" Ms. Green suggested.

"I just bought this house end of last year. I had been living in a rented duplex, but wanted my own home." Eleanor led her through the living room with its redbrick fireplace and then through the dining room and kitchen, her heart throbbing with her anxious desire to please this woman. "I chose this neighborhood because it is an established one. I don't like living where the houses are taller than the trees."

Ms. Green chuckled at this. "An interesting observation."

Eleanor showed her the three bedrooms and two baths. "This bedroom is mine. The smallest one I use as a home office and this—" she paused at the doorway of the empty bedroom "—would be my daughter's room." *Jenna's room.* "I haven't done anything more than clean and prime it because I would want to decorate it according to her wishes."

"Excellent." Mrs. Green nodded. "Why don't we go to the kitchen, and I'll ask questions, and we can fill out the rest of your application."

The interview process went quickly, and Eleanor found herself relaxing more and more.

"Now, it's not necessary to have their approval," Ms. Green said. "But I always like to know—have you discussed this adoption with your extended family?"

Eleanor nodded, her tension spiking again. "Yes, I did."

"And what was their response?" Ms. Green prompted.

"My father and aunt are very supportive," Eleanor continued even though speaking the truth clawed at her. "My mother is uncertain." That was the best description that Eleanor could come up with.

"What are your mother's concerns?"

"She doesn't understand why I want a child. She thinks I should be content with my career." Eleanor felt her hope to become a mother being sawed away from under her.

"That's not unreasonable. Many in the older generation think that a woman should delay motherhood until she is married."

Eleanor did not contradict Mrs. Green. How could she say, *My mother didn't want me, so how could she understand why I want a child?*

"I was wondering if you'd like to meet Jenna," Ms. Green asked.

"I would." Eleanor clasped her hands under the table to hide her anxious excitement.

"Jenna is on one of the Little League teams in town." Ms. Green handed her a piece of paper. "Here is the date of the next game and the time and place. Why don't you come, and I'll introduce the two of you and arrange for you to spend some time together after the game?"

As Eleanor took the paper, she couldn't hide the way her hand shook. "I'll look forward to it."

"As for your mother's uncertainty, let's hope she will come to accept your desire to adopt, but remember that's not a requirement for you to proceed." Ms. Green stood.

Eleanor rose, too. "Yes, let's." *Please, Lord. That will take a miracle.*

"Oh!" Kerry Ann exclaimed, standing up to wave wildly from her seat on the bleachers at the youth ballpark.

From beside his mom, Pete followed her gaze and saw Eleanor with her aunt and dad walking toward the bleachers at the baseball field. He rose in surprise. Why had she come?

"Miss Ellie!" Cassie squealed, charging down the bleachers to the threesome. "Come! Sit by us!" She paused to point to the team bench across from them. "That's my brother, Nicky, 'member?"

"Yes, I remember," Eleanor replied, taking Cassie's hand. With the other, she waved to Nicky, and he waved back. Then Cassie led them up to the bleacher where Pete and his mom sat. He wanted to ask why they had come, but looked to his mother. Maybe she had invited them—with matchmaking in mind?

Eleanor smiled and mouthed, "I'll explain."

He nodded, shaking hands with John and greeting Mavis. Then, as if she'd always known John, Cassie climbed up on his lap, leaving Pete and Eleanor side by side and his mother farther down, chatting with Mavis.

"Cassie has really taken to your dad," he murmured to Eleanor.

She nodded, leaning close to his ear. "I'm here to meet a little girl I hope to adopt."

Surprise rippled through him. He hadn't thought about how Eleanor might meet the child she wanted to adopt. He looked at the two coed teams and wondered which little girl might be Eleanor's.

A woman wearing jean shorts and a colorful T-shirt approached them. "Hello, Eleanor. Is this your family?"

John rose to let the familiar-looking woman enter their row and sit next to Eleanor. Pete studied her, trying to figure out who she was.

"Two of these people are my family," Eleanor replied. She motioned toward John. "This is my dad, John Washburn. And this is my honorary aunt, Mavis Caldwell. The others are friends."

"I know you," Kerry Ann spoke to the stranger. "You're Jake Green's mom."

"Yes, hi. I'm Louise Green and you're—"

"Kerry Ann Beck. Which child is yours?" Kerry Ann nodded toward the field.

"I'm here with one of my case load. That little girl with the dark brown braids and skinned knees."

Pete followed Louise's motion and picked out a child on Nicky's team. She was sitting on the team bench with her head down.

"Her name's Jenna. She lost her parents in a car accident in that awful blizzard we had on April Fool's Day this year."

"None of us will forget that storm for a long time to come," Kerry Ann said. "Didn't she have any family?"

"Unfortunately no. And none of her parents'

friends came forward to adopt. We're trying to find a good stable family to adopt her."

"Poor little thing," Kerry Ann murmured.

Pete glanced sideways at Eleanor, finding her attention riveted on the little girl. His heart went out to the orphaned child. He'd watched how his two had suffered losing only their mother. Then the urge to take Eleanor's hand nearly overcame his good sense.

Eleanor hadn't known what to expect to feel upon seeing Jenna. She'd experienced empathy over the girl's personal tragedy. But how could she have anticipated this depth and richness of longing? She wanted to run across the ball field and wrap the child in her arms.

Jenna looked up. And Eleanor's reaction strengthened. The child looked lost and lonely. Eleanor had known something of that feeling as a child. But how did it feel to be orphaned at seven years old? *Oh, Jenna, I could love you.*

Pete's arm brushed hers as he leaned forward, following her gaze. "She looks like a nice kid," he murmured.

"Yes, she does," Eleanor said, her heart awash with warm currents of caring. She tried to hide this.

The game started. Soon Nicky came up to bat. "Hit it!" Cassie called out. "Come on, Nicky!"

Nicky let two balls go by and then swung and missed. Eleanor found herself moving forward on the bench, calling out encouragement. Finally after two strikes, Nicky hit the ball and ran to first base. Their row erupted with shouts and applause.

Nicky waved from first base.

"Did you know that Eleanor played guard on her high school basketball team?" John asked, sounding proud.

"No, she never mentioned it." Pete grinned at her.

At her father's praise, her mood lifted, and Eleanor punched Pete's arm. "I bet you were on the football team."

"Guilty as charged." Pete grinned more broadly.

After two more children struck out, Jenna came to bat. Nicky had stolen second base, but Eleanor could tell that the coach of the other team expected Jenna to strike out. Perhaps because she was a girl? The thought irritated Eleanor.

Jenna swung the bat a few times getting ready and then stepped to the plate. Her posture spoke volumes about her intensity. Clearly, Jenna did not intend to strike out.

Two times the pitches were declared balls, and then two times strikes. The pitcher let loose of the ball. Jenna connected with a satisfying crack. She blasted off like a missile, short legs churning and so did Nicky.

Eleanor and Pete bounced to their feet, both shouting encouragement. "Come on! Run!"

Jenna made it to first base and Nicky to third. Unfortunately, the next batter struck out, and Nicky and Jenna's team had to hit the field again.

Eleanor watched the game avidly, calling out encouragement every time Nicky or Jenna came up to bat or were trying to run to the next base. The experience lifted her out of herself. And hearing her father and Mavis cheering on the two children only increased the joy.

Finally the game ended, and the social worker led Eleanor over to meet Jenna and her temporary foster mother. "Jenna, I want you to meet Ms. Eleanor Washburn."

While her emotions rioted, Eleanor tried to remain outwardly calm. "Hello, Jenna. You did a great job."

"But we didn't win," Jenna complained, looking unhappy. "I like to win."

Eleanor chuckled, feeling it release some of her tension. "I know the feeling. I like to win, too."

"Hey! Miss Ellie." Nicky hurried over. "I didn't know you would come to my game."

Once again, she noted that Nicky was a

handsome boy just like his dad. That thought shot through her, shocking her with its truth. "I wanted to see how you and the rest of your team were doing," Eleanor said, trying to keep from revealing her true reason for attending. She'd been warned not to let Jenna know she was considering her for adoption.

"Hey, slugger," Pete greeted his son and ruffled his boy's dark hair, which matched his own. "Not bad."

The remaining members of their group had come along to congratulate Nicky's team.

"Jenna," Ms. Green said. "Ms. Washburn is going to take you out for a while after the game and then take you home to your foster-care mom."

Jenna looked up and said politely, "Hello, Ms. Washburn."

"We call her Miss Ellie," Nicky piped up. "Dad, can we go to A&W? I'm really thirsty."

Jenna moved a step closer to Eleanor. "Should I call you Miss Ellie, too?"

Eleanor found she couldn't speak, so she nodded and brushed back Jenna's bangs.

"Can Miss Ellie and the little girl come to A&W, too?" Cassie asked, still holding John's hand.

"Why not?" Pete said. "Let's make it a party."

"But we didn't win," Jenna objected.

"We'll celebrate the fact that you and Nicky made it onto base," Kerry Ann said. "Winning's good, but A&W black cows don't only come to the winners. Am I right?"

"You're definitely right," Eleanor's dad agreed. "I love root beer floats. Let's all go!"

Ms. Green wished them all goodbye and went to her car.

Eleanor let herself be drawn into the group, heading to their vehicles and then to A&W.

The A&W was crowded, so they picked up their refreshments and drove to the nearby park. Kerry Ann, Mavis and John sat at a picnic table while Pete, his kids, Eleanor and Jenna lounged on the blanket Eleanor always carried in her car.

Eleanor was happy that Cassie and Nicky were there. Jenna chatted naturally with them about the team and about the coming school year. Eleanor forced herself not to stare at Jenna. How could she have such a feeling of connection to a child she'd just met?

Pete leaned close to her ear. "She looks like a sweet girl."

Eleanor nodded, whispering, "I can't believe that I already feel something for her."

Pete looked thoughtful. "I remember," he murmured in her ear, "how I felt when I saw each of my kids for the first time. It's powerful. I can't explain it."

His words sent chills through her.

"Eleanor," Kerry Ann said, "I've just invited your parents and Mavis to come to Sunday dinner tomorrow. About noon?"

Eleanor looked up, disconcerted. Was this a good idea? Her mother was unpredictable.

"I already accepted for us, Ellie," her dad said. He hadn't called her Ellie since she was a little girl.

That caught her breath. *A done deal, then.* "Wonderful." She pushed out a smile. "What can I bring?"

"Why don't you see if Jenna would like to come, too," Kerry Ann invited. "I'm cooking a special meal with my rotisserie grill."

"Sounds scrumptious." *And I hope my mom won't go all super-feminist on you.* Delia never curbed her tongue when confronted with a woman like Kerry Ann who had devoted herself to her family. Eleanor looked down at Jenna. "Would you like to come, too?"

"If I can." Jenna looked uncertain, as if she were trying to figure out what was going on.

"You'll like our house," Cassie said.

"We have a really neat play set, too," Nicky agreed.

Jenna nodded then, looking cheerful. "I have to ask my foster mom."

Eleanor tried not to let foreboding over her

mother's possible negativity crush the elation at meeting Jenna, a sweet girl, all alone in the world. *Lord, I could love Jenna. Don't let my mother spoil this. I want her support, not her criticism. Is that possible?*

Chapter Eight

Sunday morning had come. With one leg jiggling, Eleanor perched nervously between Cassie and Pete in the Becks' church. Jenna had not been able to come along. Maybe that was for the best since Eleanor was already on edge. Eleanor had visited this church, one of the older, redbrick buildings in town, a few times and recognized several people. Until Mavis retired, Eleanor had often driven the two hours to Madison to attend church with her.

Now Mavis sat beside Kerry Ann, smiling. Eleanor wished she could calm down and really listen to the pastor's message. But nervousness over the coming Sunday dinner at the Becks' home kept one leg bouncing. She knew her father would come to the Becks', but what about her mother? Delia never seemed to be able to just relax and enjoy people. Or just relax period.

What kept her mother wound up so tight all the time? *Especially with me?*

Everyone rose to sing the closing hymn. A guilty flush rose up her neck. She hadn't heard more than a sentence or two of the sermon, something about "loving extravagantly." *Lord, how do You want me to handle this? I'm so afraid that my mom will be cold and unfriendly to Pete's family because they're not academics like her.*

Along with the rest of the congregation as they slowly filed out of the pews, Mavis caught her elbow and leaned close to her ear. "Honey, I saw your leg jumping. Cool it. I've prayed about it. Now let God and Kerry Ann handle your mother."

Relief drenched Eleanor, Mavis's words releasing her tension in one big wave. As she joined the general exodus from the church and stepped into the hot, sunny day, she was able to greet people and wave to others. Nearby, Kerry Ann, dressed in a bright summer dress, was surrounded by people.

Eleanor joined Pete and his children, and a new worry popped up. If her mother thought Eleanor was interested in Pete, would she be rude to him? Eleanor wished she could have a mother who drew people to her like Pete's mother. Adults and children flocked to Kerry

Ann like Eastern goldfinches to a thistle feeder. The contrast between Pete's mother and her own was stark. Eleanor sighed.

As Eleanor and the others moved to their vehicles, Cassie gripped Eleanor's hand and hopped and skipped by her side. "Daddy, can I ride to our house with Miss Ellie?"

Eleanor enjoyed knowing that Cassie wanted to stay with her. Perhaps she could be like Kerry Ann, drawing people to her.

"Cassie," Pete replied, "I think that's too much trouble, moving your booster seat for such a short ride. After all, Miss Ellie is going to spend the entire afternoon with us. So just say, 'See you soon!'"

"See you soon," Cassie said without rancor.

Eleanor could only hope that under her care, Jenna would be as well behaved as Pete Beck's children were. She waved to Cassie and folded herself into Mavis's hybrid.

Soon they drove up the slope to the Beck farm, where contented black-and-white Holsteins grazed in a lush pasture. Mavis touched Eleanor's arm just before they got out. "Are you cool?"

Perceiving this had nothing to do with a low-nineties temperature, Eleanor nodded. "I'm going to enjoy myself."

Mavis gave her hearty chuckle. "I'm kind

of intrigued about how Kerry Ann will handle your mom." Her face became serious. "You know that your mom's funny ways have their root in her own insecurity, right?"

Before Eleanor could question Mavis about this revealing statement, her aunt exited the small car and was heading toward the side porch under the shade of the oak grove. Eleanor followed her, feeling the grass tickling her feet through her sandals. Like Kerry Ann, she'd worn a long summer dress from India in an exotic print of earth tones, especially a subtle green. It flowed around her, cool cotton, which breathed in the summer heat. She felt free in it.

When she turned the corner of the house, an unexpected sight brought her up sharp. "Mike?"

Wearing cutoff jeans and a black, torn T-shirt, he sat in a lawn chair beside a rotisserie. "Hey, Ellie! Looking good!"

"What are you cooking?" The scent of garlic drew her.

"A couple of legs of lamb, Armenian style. Mom's latest foray into international cuisine."

"So you became the cook?"

"Yeah, I went to Saturday night service so I could be number one chef this morning." He stretched out his full length and yawned. "It's been such hard work. You have no idea."

She laughed out loud.

Now in play clothes, Cassie and Nicky crowded around their uncle.

"It smells good, Uncle Mike," Nicky said.

At the sound of a car door slamming, Cassie turned and recognized Eleanor's dad, who was approaching. "Mr. Washburn!" she shouted, running to greet him and Eleanor's mother.

John swung Cassie up into his arms and she shrieked with giggles over something he said to her.

Delia, unsmiling and carrying a lunch-size plastic cooler, marched beside him.

At the sight of the green-and-white cooler, Eleanor blanched with embarrassment.

At the same moment, Kerry Ann came from the house onto the large, screened-in porch, carrying a tray. Following her, her husband, Harry, lofted another one.

"Come onto the porch!" Kerry Ann called. "Come sample the *mezze!* Or Armenian appetizers!"

Hiding her own pleased surprise, Eleanor obeyed her hostess and entered the porch through a screen door. "*Mezze?* Really?"

"Yes." Kerry Ann and Harry placed both platters on the long table. "I hope I made enough."

John let Delia enter first. "Wow, the lamb smells great and I haven't enjoyed *mezze* since our last trip to the Mediterranean."

Delia stood just inside the door, staring at the platters.

"Oh, Delia, you didn't need to bring anything," Kerry Ann said, motioning toward the cooler and ignoring her guest's disgruntled expression.

"I don't eat red meat or fried foods," Delia said, tight-lipped. "So I brought my own lunch."

Stunned silence.

Eleanor stared straight ahead, trying to keep her composure. Did her mother even know the definition of *tact?*

"Well, then I guess you won't get to sample my delicious leg of lamb," Kerry Ann said brightly. "But the *mezze* should be right up your alley. I have sliced cantaloupe, tomatoes, hummus, pita bread, kalamata olives—"

"And Tabbouleh!" John exclaimed. "My favorite."

"What's Tabbouleh?" Cassie asked.

"You'll love it. It's got mint and tomatoes in it."

"Mint?" Cassie asked.

John let her down and led her to the table. "Let's try some hummus on pita bread first."

"Hummus?" Cassie asked. "Do bees make it?"

John laughed out loud. "Good question. Let's

see if it takes like honey." He dabbed a bit on a pita triangle and held it out to her.

Cassie licked it. "It's not sweet."

"No, but I like it." John made one for himself and popped it into his mouth. "Come on and sit down, Delia. This is so refreshing. A real treat."

While Delia slowly, reluctantly made her way to the table, Cassie tried everything on the *mezze* platters but then only asked for seconds of the melon. John helped her serve herself.

Delia sat down beside her husband and reached for an olive. "Are you of Mediterranean descent?" she asked Kerry Ann.

Harry snorted. "No, she just takes weird cooking classes and then we have to eat what she makes." Then in opposition to his critical tone, he picked up a pita triangle and dove into the Tabbouleh with gusto.

Along with Mavis, Delia sampled the platter of various appetizers, her face disconcerted, pleasure and shock vying for prominence.

Eleanor sat down next to Cassie and began to sample the *mezze,* too. "Kerry Ann, everything's delicious." Eleanor tried to hide her satisfaction that her mother hadn't been able to insult Kerry Ann. And Delia had been shown that a farmer's wife could do more than fry pork chops or grill hamburgers. Why did her mother always assume superiority?

Eleanor glanced at Pete and caught him looking at her mother with a puzzled expression. He gave Eleanor what she thought was a smile meant to let her know he wasn't upset.

But she still wished that her mother didn't always have an agenda. And what had Mavis meant about her mother's insecurity? Her mom was strident about her independence. Didn't that mean she had almost too much confidence? And today, she'd blatantly displayed how little she cared about others she didn't deem worthy. What if she treated little Jenna like this? Cold fear trickled through Eleanor. *I won't let that happen.*

After the feast, and it had been a feast, was devoured, Pete glanced at the faces around the table. Everyone looked full and content— except for Eleanor's mom whose face appeared pinched with disapproval. What was with that woman?

"Why don't you and Eleanor take the kids outside for some fun, Pete?" Kerry Ann suggested. "Your brother Mike can help me fill the dishwasher, and then we can all just relax in the shade." She fanned herself with a small, cardboard fan from church. "The humidity has stayed so high this summer."

"You come, too," Cassie said, getting up and taking John's hand. "You come swing. It's fun."

"Okay." John rose. "Kerry Ann, you should open a restaurant. Amazing food. Delicious." He glanced down at his wife. "Wasn't it, Delia?"

"Yes, yes, it was. Amazing," Delia parroted.

Pete analyzed Delia's tone. She might be amazed, but she was not happy about it.

"Harry," Mavis said, "would you pour me another glass of that fresh lemonade? I'll take it with me. Nicky here wants to show me his fort."

With a wave of his arm, Pete invited Eleanor to join him. She rose and almost everyone trooped out of the screened-in porch.

Delia rose and walked to the screen door, stepped outside and fainted, falling to the grass.

"Delia!" John called out, turning back. Reaching his wife, he dropped to his knees. Eleanor followed, but stayed behind him.

Pete knelt beside John. "Is she breathing?"

"Yes, she's unconscious, but breathing. She never faints." John just stared at Delia.

Pete took her pulse. As a teacher, he'd been trained in CPR. "Her heart's beating, but her pulse is slow and faint. I think we'd better get her to the E.R." He rose. "Mike, help me carry Delia to Dad's car. We'll be able to lay her on the backseat."

"But won't she wake up on her own?" Eleanor said, sounding baffled.

Pete shook his head. "She might, but I'd feel better if we get her to the E.R. If she hasn't fainted before, it's a sign something's wrong."

"Yes," Kerry Ann agreed. "Pete, you drive and take John with you."

"I'll drive Eleanor." Mavis grabbed up her purse. "Come on, honey."

Soon the two cars drove up to the nearby hospital. Just as Pete parked at the emergency entrance, Delia, lying on the backseat of the older sedan, began to rouse.

John leaned over the back of the front seat, speaking to her in a low voice.

Pete rushed inside for a wheelchair, returning as swiftly. "Can she sit up?"

"Where…?" Delia mumbled, sounding disoriented.

"At the E.R," John said. "You passed out."

Delia mumbled something unintelligible.

The two men supported her out of the SUV and onto the wheelchair. John rolled it inside while Pete parked the car. When Pete arrived in the E.R., Eleanor and Mavis were speaking to the receptionist.

Pete came up behind Eleanor and rested a hand on her shoulder. "They've already taken your mom in?" he asked.

"Yes." White-faced, she turned to him. "Mother's never sick."

"Your mother never admits to being sick," Mavis said, sounding angry. "She just won't listen."

Seeing Eleanor's stricken expression, Pete kept his hand on her shoulder.

She reached up and pressed it with hers. "Thanks," she whispered.

He pulled her into a one-arm hug. "Your mom's going to be all right. I mean she just fainted. It might have been the heat and humidity."

"Let's sit down," Mavis suggested, motioning toward the nearly empty waiting room. "I'm sure John will let us know what's going on."

Time passed. Pete sat beside Eleanor and held her hand while Mavis—obviously looking for distraction—switched the waiting room TV to The Weather Channel. Pete listened to the patter about lows and storm fronts, but he focused on Eleanor. How would he feel if this was *his* mother? He couldn't imagine his vibrant mother needing medical care. He squeezed Eleanor's hand, reassuring her.

Finally John came out, looking dazed and worried. "They're running blood tests and have her hooked up to a heart monitor. She completely lost consciousness again."

Freeing her hand from Pete's, Eleanor rose and wrapped her arms around her dad.

With a grateful but worried smile, John returned a quick hug. "I have to go back, honey. As soon as I know anything more, I'll come right out. I think it's best if you wait here with Mavis and Pete."

"Okay." Eleanor released him.

Pete noticed she was blinking back tears. She sat beside him again. He claimed her hand once more and held it. "I'm sure my family's praying for her," he murmured.

Eleanor nodded, obviously unable to speak.

Oh, Lord, even if she's a difficult person, help Delia Washburn, he prayed.

Nearly an hour later, John hurried out to the waiting room. "She's in insulin shock."

"What?" Eleanor voiced the obvious question for all three of them.

"I know." John shoved his hands through his thick, silver hair. "It's just not possible. She can't have diabetes."

Pete held on to Eleanor's hand. She looked shocked and scared. He gripped her hand more firmly, trying to let her know she could count on him.

Eleanor turned to him and rested her head on his shoulder. "This can't be happening."

* * *

Eleanor stood with her father beside her mother's bed. As soon as she had been diagnosed as diabetic, Delia had been moved to a room upstairs. Two IVs had been inserted into her arm, and she was receiving insulin and fluid.

Eleanor couldn't think. She recalled one time when visiting California, she'd experienced this feeling of disorientation during an earth tremor. As things around her had shaken and she'd stumbled and nearly fell because of the floor moving under her, she'd experienced this same inability to focus.

My mother is diabetic. My mother fainted in diabetic shock. But that isn't possible.

Delia moaned and began moving her head.

Eleanor's father reached for his wife's hand. "Delia?" he said gently. "Delia?"

Eleanor took her place at her father's side, opposite the IV pole and other medical paraphernalia her mom was hooked up to. "Mom?" she whispered.

Delia's eyelids fluttered open. "Where am I?" she muttered through dry lips.

John reached for a water glass and pitcher on her bedside table. Soon he held the glass to Delia's lips. "Take a sip. Your mouth is dry."

Delia drank and cleared her throat. "Where am I, John?"

"You're at the local hospital. You passed out after lunch."

"Passed out? I never faint."

"Mother," Eleanor said, "you fainted, and you've been unconscious now for over three hours."

Delia looked at her, obviously puzzled. "I remember eating lunch at the farm. And you're right. I did faint. Must have been the heat and humidity."

"No, Delia," John countered. "You have been in diabetic shock. Your blood sugar level was three hundred and eighty-two. You could have died."

Delia stared at him, her face crunched up. Finally, she inhaled. "John, this isn't the time for joking." She moved to pull out the IV.

John grabbed her hand and wouldn't let go. "Leave that alone. Those IVs are to give you needed insulin and fluids. The doctors expect you to stabilize by tomorrow morning. And on the day after, you'll be taking diabetic training. Then I'll check you out and take you back to Mavis's house to convalesce."

Delia glared at him. "You are talking nonsense. I eat healthy foods, and I keep myself at the same weight I was before I got pregnant with Eleanor. I do not have diabetes. It's impossible."

"It's possible because you have it," John replied with steel in his tone.

Delia's expression became belligerent. "Someone in the lab mixed up my test results with someone else—"

At this critical moment, a nurse entered. "Oh, I'm so glad you've regained consciousness, Mrs. Washburn."

"It's *Doctor* Washburn. And my husband says that this hospital has misdiagnosed me with diabetes. I do not have diabetes. There has been some mistake in the lab."

Eleanor cringed at every rude word of denial.

The nurse said nothing, just turned and walked from the room. Delia sputtered in irritation.

The nurse returned to the side of Delia's bed. "I've brought a glucose monitor. Please give me your hand."

Glaring, Delia offered the nurse her free hand, still muttering under her breath about incompetence.

The nurse calmly pricked Delia's finger and let the drop of blood fall on the glucometer strip. "Mr. Washburn, would you read the number there please?"

John leaned over and read aloud, "Two hundred and thirty-one."

"Well, that's progress but we need to get her blood sugar level down below one hundred before your wife will be out of danger of further insulin shock. Or death."

Delia gawked at the woman, who went on to calmly check Delia's IV bags and readings and left with a cheery, "I'll be back with a snack."

"Now do you believe us?" John asked sternly.

Delia's mouth pinched together. Finally she said, "This is just a rural hospital. I don't have diabetes. I'm perfectly healthy."

Eleanor watched her mother fold her arms and glare at the IV pole.

"You have diabetes—" John spoke in a quiet but determined tone "—and you're staying here until they get your glucose to a healthy level, and you'll be taking the diabetic training day after tomorrow."

Delia wouldn't meet his eyes.

What would they do if Delia refused to take this seriously? Eleanor worried her lower lip.

"Hey," a voice came from the doorway. Pete stood there. "I don't want to intrude, but Mavis has gone home. She needed to feed her cat."

"What did your mother put in that meal?" Delia snapped. "She made me sick."

Everyone froze in place for a moment. Eleanor hoped Pete wouldn't try to argue with her mother. Some denial was probably normal, but her mother always dismissed everything that didn't fit what she had decreed must be reality.

"That's not true, Delia," John said. "You need to start being sensible. Now." John checked his watch. "Pete, will you take our daughter down to the cafeteria? Make her eat something. It's due to close in five minutes."

"Dad—" she tried to object.

"Please bring me back a sandwich," John said, waving her away. "And bring me something to drink. I'll be staying the night here."

"Come on," Pete said, gesturing Eleanor to come with him. "We'll have to hurry. The cafeteria's in the basement."

Eleanor walked to him and didn't look back. They hurried to the elevator, rode down two floors and then whisked through the hall to the deserted cafeteria.

"We don't have anything left to sell except what is in the coolers," the woman at the register said. "Sorry."

"I don't have much of an appetite, anyway," Eleanor admitted.

"But you need to eat," Pete said, cupping her

elbow, drawing her toward the coolers. "And your dad will need something for the long night."

She nodded and filled a tray with a variety of foods she knew her dad liked. They paid at the register, and as they walked out to the seating area, a worker pulled down the grill shutting the cafeteria for the night.

Eleanor sat at the table Pete had led her to and bowed her head, more in fatigue and despair than prayer.

Pete took her hand. "Father, bless Delia, John and Eleanor as they go through this hard time. Bless them with Your peace."

Eleanor blinked back tears, smiling at him.

"Now, pick something and start eating," he said.

Eleanor looked down at her crowded tray. She opened a salad with a chicken breast and began trying to cut up the meat. "I feel so tired."

"Emotional exhaustion," Pete said. "I know how that feels. I'd rather work sixteen hours of physical labor than worry for a day."

She'd forced herself to begin eating, so she just nodded, chewing the cold chicken.

Pete handed her a dressing packet. "Here. This might make that taste better."

She smiled and obeyed him. The ranch dressing did wake up her taste buds. And that made her think about her mother's accusation about Kerry Ann's meal being the culprit in her sickness. "I'm sorry my mother said that about your mother's cooking—"

Pete stopped her with a hand. "She's just upset. Diabetes is serious. It will probably take her some time to process. I mean they usually talk about diabetes occurring in people who carry too much weight."

"The doctor told us that this might be the result of an autoimmune reaction or a virus that weakened her pancreas. It happens."

"First time I've heard of it. Come on. Eat."

Eleanor had never felt less like eating, but she had to, or now she'd be the one fainting. She made herself take another bite and chew. The few people left in the cafeteria finished and drifted away. Even the elevator music trailed off. Just a few lights glowed over the area of empty tables around her and Pete. Finally, she couldn't make the effort to eat any more.

She put down her fork and gazed at Pete. Tears suddenly broke through and poured down. She covered her face with both hands.

Then Pete came to her side and drew her up and into his arms. He said nothing, just let her weep as she rested her head on his shoulder. She faced away, not wanting him to speak to her. She had believed in her mother's inflexible will and that her refusal to admit any weakness would hold off any illness. Mother had always been invincible. And now that had been proved false. Eleanor's world had just tilted on its axis, the same as Delia's had.

Pete stroked her hair and wonderful currents of warmth flowed from his hands through her. She didn't move, not wanting to break the connection. His comfort brought strength. She turned her face toward his.

She opened her eyes and watched his lips come down to hers, and then she was kissing him and he was kissing her.

She didn't pull away. Couldn't. His warm lips held her bound to him. Insistent, gentle, coaxing—his kiss stormed her walls and brought them down like stone to powder.

Finally the kiss, or kisses, she couldn't tell which, came to an end. Yet he kept her close to him.

"I didn't mean to kiss you," he murmured in her ear. "But you started to cry. Don't cry, Ellie. You're not alone in this."

She rubbed her face into his cotton shirt, drawing in his clean, healthy scent, giving her a sense of intimacy and connection. "I feel like I've known you forever," she whispered.

He rested his head on the top of hers. "You're easy to know."

Easy to love? She didn't know why that thought welled up from deep within, but it rattled her. "You're a good friend," she said, withdrawing from his embrace.

Better to make the move herself than wait for him to pull away. And he would. He was a caring man, but he'd been wounded by his ex, just as she had been by her two broken engagements. Why were some people lucky in love and others not?

He didn't pull back, reaching out and smoothing hair from her face. "I guess we better get this food to your dad. I don't think they'll mind us taking the tray upstairs."

Eleanor nodded and began removing the debris left from her meal. When she'd finished, Pete picked up the tray. "Let's go."

Eleanor wanted to stay here in this quiet, private place, but she knew that wasn't possible. Just as kissing Pete again wasn't possible. He'd behaved as if their kiss had merely been comfort, but she knew better.

Pete led her down the deserted, dimly lit hall to the elevator. At his nod, she pressed the button to go up.

So we're attracted to each other, I get that. But starting something now makes no sense. My mom's sick. Neither of us has a good record

when it comes to romance. I guess we were just
weak for a moment.

When the elevator door opened, she forced
herself to enter. She must stop herself from
remembering, savoring their kiss. It couldn't
happen again.

Chapter Nine

Eleanor's stomach had tied itself in so many knots she was nauseated. Swishing a lamb's wool duster, she wandered around Mavis's spotless house trying to fool herself that she was dusting—not dreading her mother's homecoming. She listened for the sound of her parents' car. Mavis and Dad were bringing Delia home from the hospital after her diabetic training. Was her mother still in denial? Would she still be angry, still refuse to do what she must to stay healthy?

Car doors slammed outside; Eleanor braced herself. She hadn't been able to visit the hospital yesterday because she had to appear in court on several cases. But that excuse should please her mother, right?

Eleanor moved to the kitchen just as Delia

stalked up the three steps into the room. "Hi, Mother. How are you?"

Delia went to the refrigerator and set something that looked like a prescription bag inside. "I'm fine."

John entered the kitchen. "She went through her training."

"Of course I did," Delia snapped. "I have diabetes. I have accepted it. But we don't need to talk about it."

Mavis stepped into the kitchen. "And we don't need to snap at each other about it, either."

An edgy silence followed this statement. Delia stared at the floor.

Frozen in place, Eleanor could only admire Mavis's bravery in the face of her mother's nasty mood.

"I just don't want everybody treating me like an invalid. I'll deal with this," Delia stated, sitting down at the kitchen table and shading her eyes with her hand. A gesture of fatigue?

"I'm glad," Eleanor said with sincerity. She sat down at the table near her mother. "But it was a shock." And the sensations she'd experienced when she'd heard the diagnosis repeated, shaking her again. *Mother, you could have died.*

"Yes, it was," Mavis spoke up, forestalling Delia, who appeared ready to take umbrage at Eleanor's words. "I'm still reeling."

Delia cast Mavis a poisonous look.

And that was the last straw for Eleanor.

"Why do you always have to act like this?" Eleanor snapped. "As if life were a battle you had to win?"

Delia stared at her.

"Why can't anything ever be easy with you?" Eleanor realized all the words she'd stored up for years were bursting through now. "You always have an agenda—like bringing a cooler to Sunday dinner at the Becks'. Why do you always assume that anyone without PhD after their name is beneath you?"

Delia looked nonplussed.

"Why do I have to be the quintessential professional woman to please you?" Eleanor shook with the strength of her emotions. "I'm beginning the adoption process. Why do I have to be afraid that you'll say something that might hurt any child I adopt? Why isn't anything I do ever enough to satisfy you? Why don't you love me?"

Trembling, Eleanor paused to take a breath and found she couldn't say another word. Her stomach knots had constricted even tighter. She nearly pressed her hand to her midsection to stop the pain. The already-strained silence tautened.

Delia stared at Eleanor as if she'd never seen her before.

Eleanor burst into tears and covered her face with her hands. She heard Delia get up and leave. From the corner of her eye, she noted Mavis following her mother, who was evidently heading to her room.

"I have to go," Eleanor said to her father, rising and wiping her face with her hands. "I'm expected at the Habitat site."

She rushed from the house, ignoring her father's half-heard words. She couldn't handle any more right now. *Why did I lose control like that?*

Not many minutes later, she parked at the curb near the Paxtons' future house. The emotional outburst had left her little energy and prone to tears. *But I'm expected.*

The tent Pete had borrowed from the school district shielded the shell. Pete along with other volunteers, lounged around, obviously finishing lunch. Kevan sat beside Pete, eating a sandwich. Her stomach growled, but she would miss a meal. Anyway, how could she eat with her stomach clenched?

She walked up to Pete and sat down. When several of the women volunteers shared conspiratorial-matchmaking glances, she realized she should have chosen to sit beside someone else. But if she moved now that would give the interested parties even more to talk and wonder about. "How's it going, Pete?"

"How's your mom?" Pete asked, ignoring her question.

"She went through diabetic training and has accepted that she has diabetes." *Sort of.*

He nodded. "It's a tough pill to swallow."

"Yeah, Pete was telling me about her," Kevan said. "Sorry to hear it."

Eleanor nodded to Kevan and smiled. Some of the words she'd thrown at her mother echoed in her mind. *I shouldn't have said all that. I'm sorry, Lord.*

Then she noticed that Pete was studying her. "It will get easier," she said, for something to say.

"Right." He swiveled to look at the shell. "I think we can get the roof sheeted today. And the walls are about done. We might as well—"

The arrival of her dad's red hybrid at the curb caught not only her attention but Pete's. He broke off and rose. "Hey! John!"

Her father had changed into work clothes, his favorite faded T-shirt and jeans. "Thought I could use some fresh air and exercise. What are we doing today?"

Seeing her dad rocked Eleanor. Fresh tears smarted her eyes. She blinked fast and sucked in air. *What's wrong with me? Why am I so emotional today?*

As Pete introduced Kevan to John, he glanced back and forth as if he were picking up on the unseen tension between father and daughter.

"Glad to have all the help we can get," Eleanor managed to say. Had her father come to scold her? Or for some other reason he wasn't saying? Was there more to her mother's condition than she had been told? "Dad, Pete tells me we're working on sheeting the roof."

"Yeah," Pete agreed. "How are you on ladders?"

"Frankly, I prefer to stay on the ground, if possible," John replied.

Kevan laughed out loud.

"You can work with my crew laying subfloor." Luis loped into sight from the back of the tent. "I'm not much for working on ladders, either."

Eleanor wondered where Colby could be, but didn't want to ask. Maybe he had to work at Dairy Queen today.

"Good deal. How about you, Ellie?" her dad asked.

She wondered why he'd started using her childhood nickname. Perhaps because Cassie called her Miss Ellie? "I can do that." She opened her toolbox at her feet and drew out her nail gun. "Have nail gun. Will lay floor."

The volunteers began gathering up the trash from their lunches, stowing it away and moving back to their work stations. Eleanor and her dad followed Luis and began laying the subflooring sheets over the floor joists and nailing them down.

Her father hovered near her as if waiting for something from her. But what? She realized she was grinding her teeth. She tried to shake off her tension. Without effect.

Several minutes passed before Eleanor decided to tackle her dad head on. "I didn't mean to say all that," she muttered near his ear in between nail blasts. "You know, at Mavis's."

"Maybe it was time you did."

She glanced at her father, surprised.

A deep crease separated his eyebrows. In contrast to the repetitive hand work they were doing, he looked intense.

"I'm just so tired," she said, timing her words to the beat of her nail gun, "of not living up to her unrelenting standards. I don't think I can even try anymore."

Her father grunted. "She demands just as much from herself."

"That's *her* business. She doesn't have the right to put it on me."

Her father nodded, not looking her way.

Eleanor wished her father hadn't come. She hadn't wanted to deal with this here and now. However, just as it had happened in Mavis's kitchen, she couldn't stop herself. "I have a right to my own life."

What had changed her ability to keep all her feelings undercover? Was it the adoption? This thought struck the mark dead on. The catalyst was the adoption. The possibility of becoming a mother herself had prompted her to address the poor relationship with her own mother. Her residual tension tightened a notch.

"If she does anything to hurt the child I may adopt—" Eleanor shook inside as she said this "—I don't know if our relationship will survive."

"She won't do anything to hurt any child you adopt," he said as if confident that his words were true. He looked into her eyes.

"Why does she always have to act like she does?" Eleanor asked. "Like she's superior to women like Kerry Ann? Like I can't be anything but a lawyer?"

Her dad stretched to his full height as if working out kinks in his back. "Your mother's mother was a difficult woman. You've heard of smother love, haven't you?"

Eleanor stilled. No one had ever spoken to her about her mother's family.

"Well, when we married at the end of high school, that was what your mother escaped. Your grandmother was set against Delia going to college, despite the scholarships she'd won with her academic excellence. Your grandmother wanted her to stay home, marry a man she'd chosen for Delia and start having grandchildren for her."

Unmoved, Eleanor listened but without any sympathy.

"I'm sorry," John continued, "that she can't relax when it comes to you—"

"Why is she letting her bad relationship with her mother ruin her relationship with me?" Eleanor heard her voice rising, but couldn't keep it low. "Why is she letting her past ruin our present? And future?"

Eleanor bent and began nailing furiously, not wanting to talk anymore. Her grandmother had died before she was born. Why was her mother letting Eleanor's grandmother dictate her life and Eleanor's? *It doesn't make sense.* Why would someone let their past wreck their present?

Near the end of the day, Pete looked down and saw his mom appear with Cassie and Nicky in tow. Kerry Ann carried a large, gallon-size thermos, and so did Nicky, although he had to use two hands to hold it a few inches from the high, uncut grass. Cassie carried a stack of plastic glasses and sugar packets in a clear bag. Pete wondered what mission his mother was on now.

"We wanted to see how the house is doing. And thought some of you might like a glass of fresh iced tea," Kerry Ann announced.

Pete, along with the other volunteers, put away their tools, moved away from their jobs and accepted the glasses of tea Kerry Ann poured from the thermoses. Everyone found a spot on the new subfloor or grass and sat down. Again, Pete wondered what his mother had up her short sleeve.

Though Pete gravitated to Cassie and Kerry Ann, he kept track of Eleanor and her dad. From his vantage point on the roof, he'd observed them speaking. Their body language had expressed discord and unhappiness. Eleanor was upset, and he'd heard enough to stir his own thoughts.

He knew he had no right to stick his nose in her business. But after holding her in his arms at the hospital and comforting her, how could he just act like nothing had happened? Even now, he couldn't forget her soft form within his arms and her tears wetting his shoulder. Her mom's illness had almost taken her down.

"Anybody going to the Fourth of July carnival on Saturday?" Kerry Ann asked.

"I am!" Cassie called out, waving her hand and jumping up and down.

"Me, too!" Nicky yelled.

Pete found himself grinning. Kids brought such zest to everything, every occasion. "Oh, I think I'll stay home and read a book," he teased.

"Daddy!" Cassie scolded. "You hafta come to the carnival."

Nicky grinned, showing that he hadn't been taken in by his dad's teasing. "Cassie, maybe you should stay home and keep Dad company," Nicky said, kidding his sister.

Cassie propped her hands on her hips and glared at her brother. "Don't be stupid."

Pete held up his hand. "Okay, okay, you persuaded me. I'll go to the carnival."

"You come, too," Cassie said, taking Eleanor's hand. "Then it'll be more fun."

Pete saw that his daughter's words had brought moisture to Eleanor's eyes. Her tears moved him, and her effort to hide them drew his support. "Yes, Eleanor, you need to come," Pete said.

"I think that sounds like fun, Cassie," Eleanor said.

"It sure does," John agreed. "I wouldn't miss it. I love carnivals."

Cassie hurried over to him and climbed onto his knee. Eleanor gazed somberly at the two of them.

Pete wished he could do something for her. She did so much for others. She deserved the best, not trouble.

"The carnival will do us all good," he said, ignoring the impulse to pull Eleanor under his arm and ask her to tell him what was bothering her.

Late in the evening, at the Fourth of July carnival, Eleanor walked beside Pete, Nicky on his other side. Cassie strolled with them, too, holding John's hand. Eleanor wished she could relax and enjoy herself, but she'd glimpsed her social worker, Ms. Green, and the woman had definitely eyed her. Why?

The sound of music from the carnival rides, the metallic pinging from the shooting range and the combined fragrances of popcorn and cotton candy filled the air. Twilight had nearly given way to darkness.

In the crush of people, they'd met the Paxtons, including Dex. The Paxtons had joined

Delia, Mavis, Kerry Ann and Harry, who had all settled on their lawn chairs in the part of the large park that fronted the small lake. They were waiting for the fireworks to be set off on the lakeshore. They would start soon.

Eleanor hadn't missed that Dex had made sure that he sat beside Mavis and that he leaned in close, speaking only to her. Her aunt's low laughter burst out once again.

"I'd like to go on the Ferris wheel," John said. "How about you kids, want to sit with me?"

Cassie and Nicky yelled their approval. The carnival atmosphere had obviously "intoxicated" them.

Eleanor, on the other hand, had withdrawn from all the noise and gaiety. So many times, she'd had to stop herself from taking Pete's hand. Pete had somehow become her focus. Was she thinking of how he'd comforted her at the hospital? She couldn't stop her gaze from drifting toward his profile no matter how hard she tried. The emotional upheaval that had started with her mother fainting at the Beck farm had not ebbed, but intensified.

Ms. Green walked past them with what must be her own family. She waved, but she still gave Eleanor "the eye." This did not help Eleanor's mood. Wasn't a prospective adoptive parent allowed to go out with friends? Her own words earlier this summer to Pete about how the adoption must take first place now replayed in her mind, mocking her. She'd just said that to have an excuse for halting any change in their relationship. Did she still feel that way?

John led them to the short line for the tall blue-and-white Ferris wheel. Soon, they were giving their tickets to the carnival worker and boarding the swaying carriages. John, with Cassie and Nicky on either side of him, entered first. Then in the next carriage, Pete waved Eleanor in first. As she sat down with a bump, the carriage swayed, and Pete landed next to her with a laugh.

She tried to smile but found it difficult to curve her worry-stiffened mouth upward. The loading of all the carriages ended in a few more minutes, and then they were riding upward. Eleanor felt her stomach lurch at the motion.

"What's wrong?" To be heard over the loud music, Pete spoke directly into her ear.

She looked at him, knowing she should smile and say, "Nothing!" Instead she grasped his large, comforting hand. "I don't know," she responded into his ear. "I just feel off-kilter."

"Is it your mom's diagnosis?"

She shrugged. "I honestly don't know."

He nodded and squeezed her hand.

On the second ascent, she leaned closer, unable to forgo the comfort she knew he'd give her. And Pete would keep whatever she said to himself. She could count on that. "I think I'm worried that my mom will be cold to any child I adopt." She couldn't go on. She pressed her lips together.

Pete looked thoughtful. "I don't understand your mom. She is an unusual woman."

Eleanor nearly snorted. "My mother always has to get in everyone's face. I was so embarrassed when she brought that cooler to your mom's Sunday dinner."

"You shouldn't be embarrassed. You didn't bring the cooler."

"I know, but I can't help how I feel," Eleanor said as the raucous carnival music swelled.

He looked as if he were digesting this. "I guess," he said finally, "I don't think that you need to worry. I mean your parents retired to Arizona, right? It's not like they live with you. And nobody's family is perfect."

His final sentence comforted her. Before she could say more, the fireworks started. The Ferris wheel turned out to be a great place to view them, even though the carriages swayed and moved up and then down. And the operator appeared to be lengthening the ride. She glanced down—no one was waiting in line, anyway.

Eleanor let herself relax. Sometime in the

midst of the fireworks, Pete's arm went around her shoulders. She rested her neck back on his arm, drawing in her first deep breath in many hours. She let herself sink into the moment— the brilliant colors bursting nearly overhead, the booming-pounding of the firework explosions, the rocking, rising and lowering of the Ferris wheel carriage, the handsome, caring man so near.

She sighed. And turned toward Pete. Her nose bumped his. She smiled and adjusted. Then she was kissing him and he was kissing her. In front of God and everybody.

When this final thought broke through to her conscious will, she pulled back.

Pete looked dazed and she felt dazed. Why did she and Pete always end up kissing?

She and Pete moved apart, not touching till the fireworks ended; the Ferris wheel ride drew to a close at the same time. When Pete helped her out of the swinging carriage, her father was looking at them with a strange expression on his face. Did that mean that he'd seen them kiss?

Eleanor groaned inwardly, resisting the urge to hide her face. *My life used to be so predictable. Why is this summer so different?*

On Monday morning, Eleanor sat at her desk, piled high with briefs and other clutter. The draw of work didn't prevent her from thinking about kissing Pete on the Ferris wheel on Saturday night. She shook her head and tried to focus on the screen of her computer.

The intercom on the desk burped to life. "Eleanor, a Ms. Green is here to see you."

"Send her in." Eleanor's stomach began agitating like a washing machine on High. She rose and pasted a welcoming smile on her face.

Ms. Green walked in and glanced around at the wall with Eleanor's framed degrees and bar association commendations. "Nice office."

"Won't you sit?" Eleanor offered with a gesture toward the chair.

Ms. Green sat and so did Eleanor. They looked at each other for a few moments.

Then Ms. Green cleared her throat. "I'm here unofficially. But I saw you at the carnival this weekend."

I saw you, too. Eleanor nodded, not trusting her voice.

"You were with Pete Beck, the building-trades teacher."

"Yes?" Eleanor answered, her voice higher than usual. "Is there a problem?"

"You're in the midst of an adoption. Is Pete aware of that?"

Eleanor wanted to say that she and Pete weren't dating, but how could she explain kissing a man she wasn't dating? She had no answer to that. She and Pete had agreed just to be friends, but friends didn't kiss on the Ferris wheel on the Fourth of July. "Yes, Pete's aware of that."

"Are you certain you want to continue with the adoption process?" Ms. Green asked, gazing down at her hands.

"I don't understand—"

"You started adoption proceedings, saying that you were ready to be a mother, and that you didn't foresee marriage anytime soon—if ever. Now I see that this might have changed. I just want to make sure you haven't changed your mind. Situations change. That's life."

Eleanor wanted to challenge this assumption, but again she couldn't without looking less than intelligent.

"I'd like you to think this over carefully. If you proceed with your adoption, and if you two are dating seriously, then it changes the mix. You wouldn't be a single mom of one, but a mom of three in a blended family. All of you would be part of the new family that would be created. You see that, right?"

"I see that." *But I hadn't looked at it that way till now.*

"As I said, I've come unofficially. Your dating would have no effect on the adoption.

And from past association, I like Pete's family. I just don't want to proceed with the adoption if you might be having second thoughts. Circumstances do change."

Eleanor didn't know what to say, so she only murmured, "I see."

Ms. Green rose. "Well, that's that. You discuss this with Pete. And let me know if there has been any change in your desire to adopt. That's all I came to say."

After Ms. Green left, Eleanor stared at the door. She sank into her chair, her head in her hand. How had she gotten herself into this situation?

I'll have to talk to Pete. We need to find out why we keep kissing. Is it mere attraction? Or something more?

Chapter Ten

Ready to discuss why they always ended up kissing, Eleanor had called Pete and asked if he had time to talk. He'd replied he'd be right over. And before she could do more than agree to that, he'd added that she should dress for berry picking. He hung up, not giving her a chance to decline.

However, berry picking sounded fun. And she thought it would be easier to discuss this touchy topic while they were doing something, rather than just sitting face-to-face. The big question still hung over her. *How am I going to say aloud, "If we said we just wanted to be friends, why do we keep kissing?"*

She was still pondering this when she heard Pete's truck drive up to her back door. Wearing a perky straw hat and faded jeans, she stepped outside carrying a plastic pail. A can of bug spray in the pail rattled with each step she took.

Pete had gotten out of his pickup to come to her door. "Hi! Glad you were free!"

Guiltily, she thought about her pending cases. But her assistant and paralegal were taking care of things at the office. And she'd work longer the rest of the week to make up for taking this time off.

"I didn't have any appointments today. And picking berries sounded like more fun than sitting in the office." She wished she felt as carefree and cheerful as she sounded. But unsure of asking him about their kissing, she felt her stomach rock and roll. Wasn't he wondering about this, too?

Hands at her waist, he helped boost her up onto the high bench seat of his truck and then hurried around to climb in himself. Soon they were driving away from town.

"I'm taking you north to a place where I always find berries," he said.

She felt the need to keep the conversation going—and not about kissing. "I'm so glad that we were able to take down the tent at the Habitat site this weekend."

He nodded. "Now with a roof, windows and doors, we have everything enclosed, so the work will go really fast. Kevan is so happy that the weather won't affect the schedule any longer."

They chatted about the Habitat project. But instead of lightening her tension, her tension leaped higher with each word, each mile, each of Pete's smiles. She fought the urge to slide to sit right beside him, grateful for the restraint from her seat belt.

Before long, Pete turned onto a county road, then a back road and finally onto a bumpy, rutted forest trail. At last, surrounded by pines that pierced the blue, blue sky like arrows on end, he parked and shut off the motor. Insects hummed and clicked in the silence, far from any house or road.

Just the two of them.

Maybe this had been a bad idea.

A stray, unruly thought teased her. What if they skipped the discussion of kissing and went straight to the kissing? This thought shocked her into moving.

"When you said an out-of-the-way place, you weren't kidding." Eleanor got down from the high seat and began spraying her hands, the back of her neck and her bare ankles with the moist, airy bug spray. Her traitorous hands trembled.

She offered the spray can to Pete and he doused himself. After all the rain they'd gotten this year, the forest would be flush with the Wisconsin state "bird," the mosquito. When they were both protected, she stowed the can in the truck and looked to him expectantly, hiding her twisting anxiety. Or trying to.

"Come with me," he said, taking her hand.

This surprised her, but she didn't, couldn't, demur. She let him lead her through the pine forest over downed logs, stepping on stones across a shallow, musical creek. Pete began whistling a tune. The sound surprised some blackbirds and they flew up, squawking high above them. The trees towered over them, taller than houses. About the time she was going to ask him how far they had to walk, he halted and motioned around.

"Here we are, a meadow in the middle of nowhere. Let's see if the berries are ripe." He let go of her hand and began moving through the lush growth of wildflowers, petite, feathery baby pines and underbrush. He walked bent over, looking down. He paused. "Got one." He held up a small, red berry.

She caught up with him.

He offered it to her, holding it in front of her lips, tempting her closer. She couldn't take a deep breath, neither could she resist. She opened her mouth like a baby bird, and he dropped it on her tongue, just flicking her lower lip with his thumb. The berry burst on her taste buds—a tart, wild raspberry.

"Yum." She relished the berry and the intimate gesture of Pete feeding her. Shivers coursed down her neck, still reacting to his casual touch. She bent over to cover her all-encompassing response to him.

"We should talk and make some noise," he said. "That's why I started whistling a way back."

She stopped in the act of brushing aside the green leaves to seek berries. "Oh?"

"My dad surprised a bear here once. That's dangerous. Fortunately the bear ran the other way. But I always talk or whistle. Black bears don't like people and aren't aggressive like Western Grizzlies. If they know we're here, they'll stay away."

Was he kidding her? "Bear? I'd heard their numbers were coming back—"

"Yeah, that's why there's an annual bear-hunting season again. Now, as you pick, talk to me."

Talk to me. It sounded like such an easy request. But what she wanted to say demanded guts. Still putting off what she came here to discuss, she asked, "Do you ever bring your kids here to pick berries?"

"I took them strawberry picking at the strawberry farm in June. Kids aren't patient enough to search for the wild berries. At the farm, the strawberry vines were full of fruit and that kept their interest."

"And domesticated strawberries are sweeter and bigger," she agreed.

Pete chuckled, and she savored the sound, glancing up.

"And juicier." Pete smiled as if he'd swallowed sunshine. "Cassie and Nicky's faces, hands and T-shirts were stained with red berry juice. And they ate four berries to every one that went in the basket. I don't think the farmer made much money on us." He chuckled easily again. As if nothing serious was on his mind.

The sound triggered her gumption. "Pete," she said, avoiding his gaze, bending low and finding a cluster of little red raspberries. "We need to talk—"

"Not just to keep the bears away?" he asked, his tone sounding a bit odd to her.

She gripped tight to her resolve. *I have to ask him this.* "Pete, we've…" Her courage failed her. She couldn't go on.

"Eleanor, what is it?"

"Pete, why did you kiss me?" She didn't glance over, afraid to look into his eyes. Then she peeked from the corner of her eye. *Well, Pete?*

After a pause, he cleared his throat. "I've

given that a lot of thought myself." He stood and gazed at her. "I don't go around kissing women indiscriminately—or at all, really."

Eleanor didn't feel capable of replying to this statement. She waited for him to go on.

Picking up his pail, he bent and began brushing the leaves and picking berries. "I've spent time thinking over what I overheard you and your dad discussing the day your mom got out of the hospital. I was on the roof and you two were below me."

Unable to think what else to do, Eleanor grabbed her pail, too, and joined him. Where was this headed? "How could you hear us in all that racket?"

"I don't know, except maybe God improved my hearing so I didn't miss something important he wanted me to know, to finally *get*. I've thought it over for a long time now. And now I need to tell you what I've realized."

Eleanor recalled that day, her anger and hurt over her mother's cold, demanding nature. She pushed it aside before it blighted this special exchange.

"'Sufficient unto the day is the evil thereof,'" Pete recited.

The words sounded familiar, but she couldn't place them. And what did that have to do with kissing? "What?"

"Matthew 6:34. 'Take therefore no thought for the morrow: for the morrow shall take thought for the things of itself. Sufficient unto the day is the evil thereof.' My mom had just repeated that to me that very morning. It's her life verse. I'd mentioned something I'd been worrying about, something that might happen, and Mom quoted the verse to me—one more time. Reminding me not to spoil today with worry about tomorrow or yesterday."

Eleanor murmured, "And?" She began picking berries again.

"And later, while high up on a ladder, I heard you two talking. I admitted to myself that I was interested in you. Then you said something like, 'So she's letting a past relationship ruin our present.'"

She paused. "Yes, my dad said my mom treats me the way she does because of her bad relationship with her own mother." Eleanor refused to look up, afraid of what else she might say. This discussion was drawing them deeper into all she feared. She picked the soft red berries, clinging to their reality.

"I can see that. And then I realized that both of us are doing the same thing as your mom. We're letting our bad past relationships ruin our chance to be together, or at least explore being together. You're not my ex-wife, and I'm not Rick."

Once again, Pete's words brought her upright. "You're right," she murmured.

"But I know I'm not ready to dive into a relationship. I just can't. I guess I want to tell you that I'm changing. But that's all I can do now."

"I understand. I talked to my social worker recently," she said, bringing up one motivation for her agenda today. "She asked me if I was dating you and if we had discussed adopting Jenna."

"Jenna? The little girl that plays on Nicky's Little League team?"

"Yes, she's the one I want to adopt." Her breath caught in her throat, silencing her. And in this moment, she knew that she had already bonded with Jenna. What would he say?

He pushed the brim of her straw hat back farther and cupped her cheek with his large hand. "That's another factor we need to consider. I don't see your adoption as a problem, but the timing just isn't right for either of us."

"Shall we just table our attraction?" She cringed at her very "lawyerly" phrasing.

Pete stared at her a long time, and then nodded. She bent to pick berries and to break their eye contact. She heard him do the same. His words repeated in her mind. They all made perfect sense, yet…

"Uh-oh," Pete murmured in her ear. "I think I see a bear."

She froze. "Where?" she whispered.

"Behind you, at the edge of the meadow."

"What do we do?" Her lips stiff, she had trouble forming words.

"Nothing. Can't outrun a bear or climb higher in a tree."

Something in his tone alerted her. She swung around.

No bear.

She swung back and punched him in the chest.

"Oh!" He yelled, laughing.

"Why did you do that?" she demanded, blushing.

"It's just the Beck sense of silliness. Sorry." He didn't look sorry at all.

She realized he'd done it to break the tension of this serious conversation. And he'd been right to do so. *I'm not ready. We're not ready. But no more kissing, Pete Beck, and I mean it.*

"I think we better start picking berries," she announced repressively.

Pete shouted with laughter. Any bear within ten miles must have heard him.

Still, Eleanor remained a little afraid to believe in the possibility of being in love again. Resentment of her own cold mother stirred and Eleanor closed that door. *My life is my life and*

*I won't keep the door shut to love just to feed
my mother's insecurities.*

That Pete and Eleanor had gathered two
buckets of the little velvety wild raspberries
astounded Eleanor. The afternoon spent laughing at Pete's silly puns and teasing had passed
in a twinkling of sunlight. Pete had used the
day to set the tone for now. They would be
friends, with perhaps more in the future. For
now, that felt right.

And on the practical level, he'd insisted she
keep her bucketful, and Kerry Ann had called
to tell her how to freeze them.

So Eleanor stood at her sink, picking out
the stems and other debris like torn leaves and
dried blossoms she'd picked along with the berries. She could hardly recall a day when she'd
felt more blessed by a friendship.

An unexpected knock sounded at her back
door. She walked to the door and opened it.

Her mother stood there.

Eleanor was so shocked, she gawked. Her
mother never came alone for a visit. "M-mother,"
she stammered.

"Good afternoon, Eleanor. I hope you have
a moment."

Eleanor wasn't a coward, but her mother's
abrasive tone nearly caused her to run and hide

in her bedroom. But what could she say? *I'm not going to let you get to me, Mother.* She stepped back and waved her mother inside.

Delia walked in and went straight to the kitchen. She sat down at the tiny table. "We need to talk."

Eleanor's buoyant mood dropped to her knees. Now what had she done wrong? Trying to bolster her resistance, she sank into the chair opposite her mother.

"I have been thinking over your words. What you said to me the day I came home from the hospital. You had never spoken to me like that before."

Yes, because I could never trust that you really loved me. The old, deep crevice opened inside Eleanor's heart. Could she bear her mother's outright rejection of her? She braced herself.

"I can't think how you could possibly think I didn't love you."

Her mother's aggressive tone didn't encourage Eleanor to open up. More than once in the past, her mother had started lectures like this. Or perhaps they were more like pronouncements about what Eleanor should or shouldn't be feeling. Mother never shared; she lectured.

Eleanor sat up straighter. *Just announcing you love me doesn't cut it, Mother.*

A sudden insight came and Eleanor grabbed it. "How have you shown me you loved me?"

Her mother's mouth drew up, into a "lemon" expression. "I don't think I need to spell that out to you. My goal for you, Eleanor, was, and is, strength. Not some syrupy affection that would make you weak."

"Everyone has weak moments." Eleanor didn't know where these words were coming from. "You fainted at the Becks' house. Everyone has weaknesses."

Her mother visibly bristled.

Eleanor forestalled her by continuing, "I am not a weak woman. And I do not see loving as weakness but as strength."

"I wanted you to be free of my interference, any encumbrances. I didn't want to make you feel guilty for pursuing your goals."

"I am pursuing my goals. My goal now is to adopt a child. I don't view her as an encumbrance. Why can't you support me in this?"

"I never said I didn't—"

"You asked me why would I want to tie myself down with a child." Eleanor held in her temper.

"Well, why would you? This is the time of your life where you should be traveling, doing things you want to do."

"I want to adopt Jenna." Eleanor decided in

for a penny, in for a pound. She wanted to declare her independence on all fronts. "And Pete Beck and I may have feelings for each other."

Delia threw up both hands in a gesture of frustration. "I knew that man was behind this."

"I had begun the adoption process before I ever met Pete Beck. And we're not pursuing a relationship now. We just admitted the truth to each other."

This silenced her mother.

The two of them faced each other. Delia didn't look happy, and Eleanor knew her face must reflect the same dissatisfaction.

Finally, Delia rose. "I just don't understand you. I've done everything I could to make it possible for you to be successful and independent. And you want to throw that all away—"

"Why does adopting Jenna make me less successful or less independent? What if Pete and I do form a bond in the future? What is your yardstick, Mother, for measuring a person? A life?"

In the taut silence between them, the phone shrilled.

Eleanor rose and picked it up. "Eleanor Washburn."

"Ms. Washburn," a slightly familiar voice said, "Rhinelander police. We got two kids down here, holding them pending investigation. They say that you're their lawyer."

"What are their names?"

"Colby Miller and Luis Esteban. We tried to tell them they didn't need a lawyer yet—"

"I'll be right down." Eleanor hung up. "Mother, I have to go. It's a case."

Delia shook her head and pursed her lips. Lifting her hand in farewell or defeat, she departed.

Eleanor let her go without another word. She didn't know how to handle her mother's disapproval except to go through with her plans to adopt Jenna and for in the future to let a possible relationship with Pete develop. What else could she do? *It's my life.* Eleanor snagged her purse and headed for her car.

No matter how many times she went, Eleanor never enjoyed the police station. And never before had she represented clients while dressed for picking berries. But she didn't really care today. The effect of speaking with Pete and then her mother had made her impervious to such things. If Colby and Luis wanted her right away, they'd take her as is.

She wondered if she should call Pete. She knew how concerned he was about their future.

She decided to wait till she'd assessed the situation fully.

Upon arrival, and before she met with Luis and Colby, she talked to the officer who'd brought them in. At his cluttered desk, he explained that there had been a disturbance behind one of the convenience stores on State Highway 47. She noted how he looked at her; he was obviously disconcerted by her berry-stained fingers and casual clothing.

Luis and Colby had been picked up, running from the scene. Bottle rockets set up to be ignited and empty beer bottles had been scattered behind the store Dumpster.

Eleanor sighed. She'd used this call as an excuse to break off that uncomfortable conversation with her mom, but this didn't sound pressing. "You just saw them running from the scene?"

The officer shrugged. "I picked up evidence and will be checking for fingerprints. You know how it is. I have to pick up anybody at the scene that looks as if they might have had anything to do with what was going on or who might have been a witness. Then we start investigating."

"So this is just about illegal fireworks and alleged underaged drinking?" *And just general stupidity?* Relief trickled through her. She hadn't been looking forward to telling Pete that the two teens were in custody. He so wanted these two to make it. He'd be so disappointed if they were charged for doing something so dumb and in broad daylight.

"Yeah, you can go in and talk to them if you want." He motioned toward the door. "I wouldn't have bothered you till after we tried to match their fingerprints, but they insisted. You just got the other Miller boy clear of those burglary charges, didn't you?"

She nodded. "Since I'm here, I'll talk to them."

The officer accompanied her to the questioning room. When she entered, he closed the door behind her, and both Luis and Colby jumped to their feet. "Thanks for coming," Colby said, sounding worried.

She waved them to sit down. "Why were you two running away from the convenience store?"

"We were walking home since nobody came to get us after work," Luis said sourly.

"We heard some firecrackers and walked behind the convenience store to see who was doing it," Colby continued.

"And then the police car zooms up the alley, and we just ran." Luis looked upset. "Is this gonna get us into trouble? We just got registered for classes this fall at the community college and—"

"If you didn't do anything wrong, nothing is going to happen. Are your parents expecting you home?"

Both teens nodded. "We weren't doin' nothing," Luis muttered.

Eleanor asked them each in turn for their home phone numbers. She left a message for Colby's mom and talked to Luis's mother, explaining that the boys were being held for questioning and that no doubt they would be home late for supper.

Eleanor called her office to check on other cases. She hated the dismal questioning room, but didn't want to leave the two agitated, worried teens alone. She'd wait for the fingerprinting to be done.

About an hour later, the officer she'd spoken to earlier entered. "You two can go. We didn't find your prints on any of the evidence."

The two teens leaped to their feet, obviously ready to start berating the officer.

Eleanor forestalled them with a razor-sharp glance. "Thank you, Officer. I've instructed my clients that in the future, they should not run from a policeman. That only causes them to look guilty."

"You got that right," he said. "Come on, guys. You're free to go."

"How're we going to get home, man?" Luis snapped.

"Luis," Eleanor scolded. "As a law-abiding citizen, you should show respect to those who protect you. And if you ask me nicely, I'll drop you both off. Thank you, Officer, for being so efficient."

The cop grinned at her and motioned her to precede him out the door. Eleanor led the two grumbling teens out the front door to her Trailblazer. Soon, she was dropping them off at their houses.

Before each one got out, she warned, "Let's not do this again, okay?"

Both mumbled their thanks and scurried inside.

Eleanor continued toward home, feeling that some progress had been made with them.

Her phone rang again. She listened and smiled. "Of course I can make it. Thanks, Ms. Green." Now she knew when she might see Pete again. She hummed all the way home.

Sitting on the bleachers, Pete felt like a cat on a sizzling-hot tin roof. Would Eleanor come to watch Jenna play? Two days had passed since they'd gone berry-picking. He'd been busy with assistant coaching, getting his kids ready for the school year and preparing his own upcoming fall term. Being honest with her had been the right thing to do. Yet seeing her again felt awkward.

As he watched his son's team play baseball, his right leg insisted on jiggling. His mom kept glancing at it and trying to hide a smirk. He refused to say anything to her because he didn't want to hear what she had to say. His mother didn't miss much.

Images from berry picking with Eleanor flitted through his mind. Since then, he'd been assaulted by fresh misgivings. Eleanor was not Suzann, but could he find the strength to let go of the past completely, absolutely? That would take a long time and a lot of work.

Eleanor waved to him as she walked toward him. He stood and waved back. Then realized that he'd just announced to half the town that he and Eleanor had a thing going on.

The faux pas committed, he went ahead and strode down the bleachers and met her as she skirted the field. "Hey," he greeted her.

"Hey," she replied. "How are Jenna and Nicky doing? I was in court and then had to go home to change."

He thought she looked great in jean shorts and a pink T-shirt. He directed his mind to the game at hand. "You didn't miss much," he said, leading her toward where Cassie and his mom sat. "Did you get my messages?"

"Yes, just this morning. A few of my cases just kind of took over my life, and I've done nothing but go to and from court and my office."

"Thanks for helping Colby and Luis." Sincere gratitude crested within him.

"No problem. I'm glad to hear they were men enough to let you know."

When they arrived, Cassie jumped up, reaching for Eleanor's neck. Eleanor bent low to receive Pete's daughter's welcome hug and return it. "Hey, Cassie. Hi, Kerry Ann."

His mom beamed at them, and when Eleanor turned to sit, she avoided looking at him.

Doing the same, he sat down beside Eleanor. They watched the fumbles and fun on the field, leaping to their feet from time to time to encourage Jenna or Nicky to run.

Pete realized that Eleanor's enthusiasm added even more zest to the experience. He'd missed having someone to share this with, someone who loved children... Eleanor was a woman capable of love and commitment; she already loved Jenna. He could tell this in the way she said the little girl's name.

He watched Jenna go up to bat. What did it feel like to lose one's family at such a young age? The question tugged on his compassion, releasing it in a warm rush. Poor kid.

Then he glimpsed some people he hadn't expected arrive. Mavis, John and Delia sauntered toward them, skirting the field. Concern clutched his stomach and squeezed—hard. Delia's face was a mask except for her eyes, which sought him out immediately. Their gazes made contact. And the connection crackled. Delia did not like him. He refused to look away.

The threesome walked up the steps to join them. He sensed Eleanor tense beside him.

She lifted her chin. "Hi, Mother, Dad, Mavis."

Mavis and John greeted everyone, apologizing for their late arrival. Delia said nothing but nodded and sort of smiled at his mom.

Kerry Ann leaned toward Delia. "I'd ask how you are feeling, but it's obvious that you're doing fine."

Delia looked perplexed then said, "You're right. I'm fine." Then she turned toward the field.

Once again at the plate, Jenna managed to hit the ball and headed to first base. Everyone on their bleacher rose, cheering her on. She reached the base with several seconds to spare.

"That girl has talent," John said. "It's going to be fun attending athletic games again."

"Uh-huh," Mavis agreed.

Delia remained silent.

Pete turned his mind away from wondering what Eleanor's mother was thinking, or worse, what she might say. *Hang in there, Ellie.* Too soon the game ended.

They all stood. "Jenna is coming home with me to spend the night," Eleanor announced.

"Let's go collect her and Nicky," Pete said. They started down the bleachers.

"Eleanor!" Mavis called as the threesome headed toward the parking area. "Bring her to supper. I'm making spaghetti with meatballs. Your favorite!"

Eleanor paused, casting a questioning look at Mavis.

Pete tried to figure out whether this would please Eleanor or not.

"Okay. What time?" Eleanor asked.

"About six." Mavis waved, and John ushered the two ladies toward the parking area.

Pete decided Eleanor must be concerned about her mother's reaction to Jenna. "Don't worry," he murmured in her ear. "Your dad and Mavis will make Jenna welcome."

She cast him a grateful glance. They reached

the children, milling around the volunteer coaches. Nicky turned to him.

Jenna came over to Eleanor. "Hi. My foster mom told me you were having me over for the night. I brought my duffle bag." The girl lifted the dusty, navy-blue bag.

"Yes, we're going to have fun," Eleanor said, smoothing back Jenna's bangs. "Let's go." Eleanor smiled, but her lower lip trembled.

Pete wished he could encourage Eleanor somehow, but couldn't think of doing more than giving her a smile.

"How come she gets to go with Miss Ellie, and I don't?" Cassie demanded, pouting.

"You'll have your turn, Cassie," Eleanor said. "But tonight is Jenna's turn."

"Are you friends with her foster mom or something?" Nicky asked, his expression twisted with his trying to figure this out.

"She might adopt me," Jenna said softly.

"Yes, we're going to see if we're a good match," Eleanor said brightly. "See if Jenna can put up with me."

"You mean she will be your girl," Cassie asked, not looking happy.

Pete stooped to be at eye level with his daughter. "Jenna lost her parents this year. They died in a car crash. So she needs a family." He hoped to enlist Cassie's caring heart.

"Oh," Cassie said, looking serious. "I don't got a mama, either, Jenna."

"You don't?" Jenna appeared surprised and concerned.

"No," Nicky spoke up abruptly, as if he didn't want this discussed. "She stayed in Las Vegas, and we moved back here to live with Grandma and Grandpa."

"Oh." Jenna looked puzzled but didn't ask for any further information.

Then all of them headed toward the parking area. Kerry Ann drew the children forward, talking about the game.

Eleanor leaned toward Pete's ear. "Wish me luck…with my mom and Jenna."

He bent closer, too. "I can't see anybody—" he didn't add aloud *even your mother* "—being impolite or unwelcoming to Jenna. She's a sweet little thing."

Eleanor gave him a brave smile.

They walked Jenna and Eleanor to her Trailblazer and then headed to Kerry Ann's SUV.

His mother said under her breath, "We better pray about Eleanor and Jenna's supper at Mavis's house."

Pete nodded in reply and started praying.

God, help Ellie and Jenna. Help Delia find some love in her heart for Jenna. And not for the first time, he thanked God for the parents he'd been given.

Chapter Eleven

Tightly strung, Eleanor led Jenna by hand up to Mavis's side door. The humidity remained distinctly uncomfortable. Dabney, Mavis's cat, greeted them, winding around their ankles and purring.

"Can I knock?" Jenna asked.

"Of course." Having Jenna with her made Eleanor feel as if she were in a waking dream. She was well aware that Jenna must be on her best behavior just as Eleanor was herself. But her love for this child seemed to expand moment by moment, making it hard for her to even let Jenna leave her sight. If only Eleanor could trust her mother to show Jenna kindness. Concern about that tightened the muscles around Eleanor's mouth, making it difficult for her to smile.

Jenna stood on tiptoe and knocked, using the

new, bright brass knocker shaped like a dove of peace in flight.

Eleanor had been concerned before about her mother's reaction to Jenna. These brand-new, maternal feelings only heightened that, bringing out the mother-bear-protecting-her-cub in Eleanor.

Delia opened the door. Mavis's cat, Dabney, scurried inside. "Hello!" Delia was smiling, genuinely smiling, in welcome.

Eleanor froze in place. Her mother so rarely smiled that it was unsettling. "Mom," Eleanor stammered. "You saw Jenna at the ball park."

Bending, Delia offered Jenna her hand. "Hello, Jenna. I'm Eleanor's mother, Delia. You can call me by my name."

"Hi, Delia." Jenna added a shy little wave.

"Come in," Delia invited.

Apprehensive and confused, Eleanor let Jenna follow Delia, and the three of them headed into the kitchen, redolent with Italian spices and garlic butter. Mavis stood at the stove, just now adding the dry spaghetti noodles to a boiling pot of water. "I hope you two are hungry. Because I'm making a potful!"

Jenna waved at Mavis. "Hi, I'm Jenna."

Mavis finished her task and turned to Jenna. "I'm Mavis." She bent to grasp both Jenna's hands in her plump, brown ones. "I'm Eleanor's honorary aunt, so you can call me Aunt Mavis or Auntie. How's that?"

Jenna smiled, evidently responding to Mavis's natural warmth. "I'll like having an auntie."

"I'll like that, too." Mavis leaned down and kissed Jenna's forehead.

Her father put down the paper he'd been reading at the table. "And, Jenna, I'm Eleanor's dad, John. What would you like to call me?"

"If you're Miss Ellie's dad," Jenna said cautiously, "then you would be my granddad, right?"

"Want to call me granddad? Or grandpa? Or John is okay, too."

"Grandpa." Jenna went over to him and tentatively shook his hand. She frowned.

"What is it?" John asked.

"My foster mom told me that Miss Ellie wants to adopt me," Jenna replied, her eyes downcast, "but that I have to visit her and then live with her for a while before that happens. What if I don't get adopted?"

Before Eleanor could speak, Delia spoke up, sounding upbeat. "I can't think why Eleanor wouldn't adopt you. I think they just say that in case something really strange happened."

"In any case, Jenna," John said, patting Jenna's thin shoulder, "even if you didn't get adopted, we can still be your friends, and you can call us what you decide today. We don't have any kids in our family, so we could use one."

Jenna looked relieved. "Great. I mean that sounds good."

Eleanor's fears began to melt.

"Want to help me set the table, Jenna?" Delia asked.

Eleanor thought her eyes might pop out like in a cartoon.

"Sure," Jenna agreed. "I set the table all the time."

"Good. Let's carry the dishes and flatware out and get everything done nice in the dining room. It looks like rain, or we'd set up outside on the picnic table." Delia and Jenna gathered the tableware and left the room.

Eleanor sank into the chair at the small kitchen table, her tension leaking from her every limb. She looked questioningly at her father.

He shrugged as if to say, *I don't know what's going on, either.* Mavis just grinned and turned back to stir the noodles.

The casual supper went easily. Jenna enjoyed the spaghetti and chatted about her baseball team and swim lessons at the park district pool. Eleanor kept up her part of the conversation, but mostly listened. Her parents told Jenna about their house in Arizona. The archeological dig, taking place now in Utah, especially captured Jenna's interest. She asked many good questions.

"I know what we should do now," Mavis said, grinning. "There's a new Disney movie on in Rhinelander. Why don't we go?"

"Ooh," Jenna crowed. But then sobered. "I don't have to go." She looked at Eleanor. "If you don't want to."

"I think it's a fine idea." Eleanor expected her mother to decline.

"I haven't seen a Disney movie in forever," Delia said. "I used to enjoy taking Eleanor when she was little. My favorite was *Snow White and the Seven Dwarfs*."

Eleanor choked back her surprise. And suddenly she did remember going to the movie to see this as a child. "I remember that."

Delia gave her a self-satisfied look and took Jenna's hand. "Let's go wash our hands. Then if we get hungry at the movie, we'll be able to eat popcorn."

Eleanor still couldn't quite believe this had happened. She didn't know what had caused this change. She only hoped this new, improved version of her mother would continue.

* * *

Pete dashed through the rain, each of his children attached to one of his hands. Dripping, they ducked under the marquee and stopped at the ticket window. They paid and sauntered into the lobby where the fragrance of buttered popcorn hit them full in the nose.

"Hey, Daddy, it's Miss Ellie!" Cassie called out and began waving madly at Eleanor, surrounded by her family and holding Jenna's hand.

Suddenly Pete "got" why his mom had suggested that he take the kids to a movie this rainy evening. She probably knew Eleanor's family had planned to come tonight. But complain, not him—unless this upset Eleanor's plans. How could he convey that to her? And more troubling, or at least chancy, her mother lurked at Eleanor's side.

Would his presence give her something to complain about? Cause a scene? Hurt Eleanor's feelings? He gave up trying to figure everything out and just smiled.

John waved him over. "Why don't we let the women take the girls inside and get seats while *we guys*—" John winked at Nicky "—manage the popcorn and drinks?"

Nicky beamed at John and gave him a high-five slap. Pete chuckled. He gave Cassie her ticket and let her join the females as they moved into the theater.

"How are things going with Jenna?" Pete asked John under his breath.

"Smooth sailing so far." They bought five huge tubs of popcorn. And since the kids behind the counter recognized Pete from high school, they squirted the butter lavishly over each tub. He grabbed extra napkins to deal with this largesse, and the guys got to their seats just as the feature presentation blared to life.

Pete noticed that the seat next to Eleanor had been noticeably left open for him. Feeling a bit more conspicuous, even in the dark, he settled down beside her and offered to share his tub of popcorn with her. Jenna and Mavis were sharing a tub, so she smiled shyly and dug in.

His lips next to her soft ear, he teased, "I don't share my popcorn with just any girl."

She threw a kernel at his nose and then grabbed another handful. "I hope you brought napkins," she said and then began to chew. Her eyes widened. "How much butter did they squirt on this?"

Pete relaxed into the comfortable seat, more comfortable because Eleanor sat beside him. When they'd emptied the popcorn tub, he held hands with her. As they watched the cartoon hero and heroine fall in love, he couldn't remember feeling so happy in a very long time. Finding Eleanor was like finding the perfect fit, and that made everything feel in its proper place. They didn't have to act on their attraction. That was all in the future. Even if their relationship remained just friendship, what was wrong with that? *Thank you, Father. I feel Your hand in this. I didn't think I'd ever heal. Sorry for that.*

Later, Eleanor stood in the doorway to the room she hoped would be Jenna's. She'd bought a twin bed and made it up with pastel blue-and-white linens. "I thought I'd let you pick out the paint color for this room."

"You mean this would be my room?" Jenna asked, standing by the bed in the almost empty room. She wore her pink-and-white Hello Kitty cotton pajamas and had just brushed her teeth.

Suddenly choked up, Eleanor nodded.

"When can I come live with you?"

Eleanor's joy hit the ceiling. "As soon as Ms. Green finishes all the paperwork. Then you'll move in here as my foster daughter while the adoption papers go through."

"So you'd be my second foster mom, but you'd become my real mom?"

Eleanor nodded, unable to speak. Love for this child filled her to overflowing.

Jenna looked down as if in deep thought. She looked up. "You were sitting beside Nicky's dad at the movie, and eating his popcorn."

Not expecting this, Eleanor took a deep breath. "Yes, Pete Beck and I are…just friends."

Jenna again appeared to consider this, her expression intent. "Then you two aren't going to get married?"

Leave it to a child to get straight to the point. Thinking this might turn into a long conversation, Eleanor waved Jenna to get into bed, and then she sat down at the foot. "I have feelings for Pete, and he has feelings for me. I think we may have a future together. But that might come or it might not."

"But what about me?" Jenna sounded worried.

Eleanor smoothed back Jenna's bangs. "Pete loves kids. If we would sometime, in the future, get married, we'd be a family."

"A family?" Jenna looked and sounded as if this were not to be believed.

Eleanor nodded, cupping Jenna's soft cheek. "Try not to worry about this. I want to adopt you. Pete is good with it. Like my dad said today—even if something weird happened, we'll all still be in your life as friends."

"But I want you to be my family."

The words unleashed Eleanor's deepest emotions. She didn't know if she should or not, but she followed her instincts. She pulled Jenna to her and hugged her. "Don't worry. Everything will work out right. When Ms. Green showed me photos of children available to adopt, I knew you were the one for me. I knew it at first sight. You see, I prayed for a little girl, and here you are."

Jenna clung to her.

Eleanor sensed the child was wrestling with her own sad memories and tender hopes. *I want us to be a family, too, Jenna. I want to build a family. God bless us.*

Later, after putting his kids to bed, Pete shuffled down the stairs and walked into the living room, not ready for sleep. His mom was reading a book while the continuing rain poured down the windows. Growing darkness was closing off the view of the oaks around their house. His dad was reading an agricultural magazine and looking unusually grumpy. The atmosphere in the room could only be described as tense.

Kerry Ann looked up. "How was the movie?"

Pete couldn't stop his grin. "We just *happened* to run into Eleanor and Jenna there. Lucky coincidence?"

His mother smirked. "Mavis just *happened* to mention they'd be going tonight."

His dad sort of growled and flung a dark look at them. The difference between his optimistic mother and his pessimistic father kept their home lively. After forty years, Pete thought his dad ought to finally catch on that his mom's view of life made for a better outlook, better outcome. For a moment, he pondered the fact that his parents had been married for forty years. Their party had been planned, and the invitations had gone out weeks ago. He tried to keep from smiling.

"What do you think of Jenna?" Kerry Ann asked. "Cassie was telling me about her this afternoon."

"Who's Jenna?" Harry grumbled.

Pete sank onto the sofa. "Eleanor is planning on adopting Jenna, a little girl who plays on Nicky's Little League team."

Harry lowered his journal. "But that lady lawyer isn't married. Why would anybody let her adopt a child?"

His dad's words aggravated Pete, but he didn't let this show. "Single women and men adopt children nowadays. Eleanor will make a wonderful mom."

His dad's expression soured more. He lifted

his journal, shook it and supposedly went back to reading.

Then Pete noticed a little, furry face peeping over the arm of his mother's chair. This shocked a comment from him. "A cat in the house?"

His mother chuckled, lowered her book and picked up the grayfur ball that just fit in her hand, showing it to Pete. "Mama-cat must have just finished weaning her latest litter. This afternoon, she brought this baby to me. Carried her from the barn and meowed at the back door till I came to see." His mom stroked the kitten's head. "Isn't she sweet?"

"Cats belong in the barn," his dad muttered.

Kerry Ann found his comment amusing and tried without success to hide this. "Mama-cat has never done that before. I haven't figured out why she's done it now. I think I'll call Dr. Jake, the vet, tomorrow and see what he thinks."

Pete leaned over and, using just his index finger, stroked the tiny kitten's head, too. "Do you think she's not strong enough to survive in the barn?"

"I don't know. Maybe I should take her in to Dr. Jake—"

"Wasting money on a barn cat." With this pronouncement, his dad got up and left the room.

Kerry Ann sighed. "I love your father, but sometimes he can be a big, old grump."

Pete grinned. "Really? I hadn't noticed."

His mom shook her finger at him, scolding even as she grinned impishly. She sobered. "You looked very 'together' with Eleanor at the game today."

"Guilty as charged." To forestall any forthcoming questions, Pete rose and went to the kitchen.

His father was standing at the window, glaring out at the rain. From the set of his shoulders, Harry looked miserable. But Pete knew from experience not to try to cheer his dad up. That was Pete's mother's department. Pete opened the fridge to get something to drink.

The phone on the wall rang. Pete answered it with the family name, "Hi, the Beck house."

"Uh, I, uh…"

"Yes?"

The person hung up.

This didn't happen very often. Pete looked at the receiver as if it would tell him what was up. Then, trying to identify the caller, his mind replayed the brief series of syllables. He gripped it tighter, rattled. *No, it couldn't have been. It couldn't have been* her *voice.*

Two days later, Eleanor glimpsed Pete striding toward her at last. She'd been anxiously waiting inside the doorway of the Paxtons' future home for Pete to arrive. Kevan had already arrived and was drilling in wall board with a few other volunteers. Even with everyone milling around behind her, she was tempted to throw her arms around Pete. Mentally, she took a step back. She had so much to tell him about her weekend visit with Jenna.

"Hey!" he greeted her. "Sorry I haven't called. Life just got super busy on the farm. What's on the agenda today?"

She kept her "boss" identity in place, but it wasn't easy. His dark hair needed a haircut and beckoned her to finger it into place. She resisted the impulse. "The plumbing and electrical have been inspected and we're insulating and drywalling today."

"Fun. By the way, I wanted to invite you—"

Before he could say more, Luis and Colby surged inside right behind him. "Hey. We made it."

Eleanor shook her head at them, smiling.

"My mom wants to have you two over for dinner," Colby said, "for getting the charges against Danny dismissed. And for going down to the station about those bottle rockets and beer bottles."

"Your mother doesn't have to do that," Eleanor said, not missing the fact that she and Pete were being invited as a couple. The Hope,

Wisconsin, grapevine must be alive and active these days. Without meaning to, she moved closer to Pete. "Your brother is paying me for my services."

"Yeah, but Mom says you can't pay for kindness with money."

Eleanor felt herself color. "I was just doing what was right."

"That's something else no one can pay for with money," Pete said.

Eleanor wondered what Pete wanted to invite her to. It couldn't be the fortieth anniversary party because she'd already received her written invitation, which had made it very, very clear that the party was intended to be a surprise!

"Hey!" Kevan appeared just behind Eleanor in the open doorway. "This house isn't going to get built if people stand around yakking." His broad smile belied his criticism.

"We're here! We're ready!" Luis saluted, making Kevan burst out laughing.

"Glad to see they are getting the message about walking the straight and narrow way," Pete whispered in her ear, making her shiver in the summer heat.

Eleanor and Kevan gave way so Pete and the teens could enter. She wished for a moment alone with Pete but resigned herself to not getting one—now. *Just as well.*

She watched Pete joking with Kevan, and then he buckled on his work belt and began working. She couldn't keep her eyes from watching the confident way he moved. Every motion was calculated for efficiency and accuracy. He got the crew insulating quickly and self-assuredly.

She turned at last and picked up her own cordless drill. *We'll talk later and see what I'm being invited for.* She could wait. Her cup of love and happiness overflowed already.

Heart beating with anticipation and apprehension, Pete, with Nicky and Cassie in the rear seat, drove up to Eleanor's house. Pete got out and went to knock. Opening the door, Eleanor appeared. He could hardly take his gaze from her, so beautiful in a yellow blouse and matching shorts. With her long tanned arms and legs, she looked like summer in human form.

Jenna shyly waited just behind her. Pete had invited them both to the picnic on the American Legion Campground to benefit an area family who needed help with medical bills.

Pete's stomach occasionally did a little hop and jump. This would be the first time that Eleanor and their kids would appear in public altogether. And he'd explained to Nicky and Cassie that he and Miss Ellie weren't dating but that Miss Ellie was planning to adopt Jenna and he wanted to help Jenna feel good about this and feel welcome.

Kids were always unpredictable. How would the afternoon go? Would the three children pull together or decide to squabble?

All this could explain why his children waited so seriously and quietly in the backseat of his extended crew cab. "Ready to go, ladies?" he asked Eleanor and Jenna.

"Yes, we're ready." Eleanor sounded as if she'd just run a race and won, excited and breathless.

He grinned, recognizing the same feeling within himself. Sometime in the future, they might be a family of five. Right now he and Eleanor would be working on establishing their friendship on a strong foundation with a future goal of blending the three children into a possible family. He inhaled deeply. A plenty big enough job for now.

Lingering acid bitterness over his divorce tried to leech into his heart. He refused to let it. The past was past. Eleanor and Jenna were the present for him, Cassie and Nicky.

Jenna climbed into the back, saying shy hellos to his kids who responded in kind.

Clasping his hands on her waist, he swung

Eleanor up onto the high seat. Despite cautions, elation lit his heart.

She laughed out loud, giving sound to his own joy. Then, after he stowed her bowl of salad in the large cooler in the rear, he climbed in and off they went, driving to the thick, green forest nearby with its many lakes.

When they arrived at the picnic site, gray clouds were already racing overhead. Probably yet another storm was blowing in. The instant he helped Eleanor down from the pickup, they were the object of general attention—as he'd expected. Everyone turned to study the five of them, speculating about the arrangement, no doubt.

"Oh, look, the Paxtons have come, too," Eleanor said, gazing behind him.

He turned and saw Kevan, Jenelle and Tiesha looking ready for summer fun. Just behind them, Kevan's Uncle Dex and Eleanor's Aunt Mavis walked side by side. He sent Eleanor a sideways, conspiratorial glance concerning this twosome.

She winked back at him and whispered, "Love is in the air."

He laughed out loud but tried to cover it by raising his hand and welcoming Kevan's family. Together, they moved to the center of the bustling fundraiser.

He and Eleanor wrote generous checks to the benefit family, bought activity tickets for the various games and added their bowls of two kinds of salad to the tables already piled high and wide with donated food. The Paxtons followed suit.

As they strolled through the park, Pete introduced the Paxtons and Mavis to friends who came up to greet them. His friends appeared torn between welcoming the new family and obviously trying to figure out what was going on between him and Eleanor. He just smiled. Laughter and friendly voices surrounded them.

Eleanor and he followed the children to the bean-bag throw. There, two of his old high school buddies had to be introduced to Eleanor. Pete put up with their veiled teasing. Nothing could bother him today.

Then the five of them moved on to the hula hoop area.

"Can you hula hoop?" he asked Eleanor.

"I've never tried," she replied.

"Well, I'll teach you, then." Pete handed in a few activity tickets and accepted the first of the colorful hoops.

She laughed. "Better help Jenna and Cassie first."

Soon he was busy settling the plastic hoops around the girls' waists. Jenna managed to keep it up for a few minutes, but not a crestfallen Cassie. Pete let Eleanor comfort her.

Eleanor stooped and spoke softly to Cassie. "You're just too close to the ground yet. When you're a bit bigger, it will work."

"Do you still like me?" Cassie asked, glancing at Jenna who was barely keeping her hula hoop above her hips.

"Of course. Nothing can change my liking you. Certainly not a hula hoop."

"But she—" Cassie swung her head toward Jenna "—can keep it up."

"She's taller than you are. That's all. You're my Cassie and always will be." She hugged Cassie. "Now, come on. It's my turn to try." Eleanor rose, nodding toward Pete.

Pete dropped a hula hoop over her head. "Let's see how you do."

She swung the hoop and began to sway and swing trying to keep it up. Gravity won; she lost. She lifted it again and tried again and again.

Cassie began giggling, and soon everyone was giggling.

Finally, Eleanor gave up, letting the hoop clatter to the grass. "I'll stick to law."

The five of them moved on to watch the horseshoe-tossing competition. *Clink, clink* sounded with each toss. The sky overhead darkened. A hammerhead cloud loomed in the distance towering over the tops of green trees.

Eleanor looked up, worried. "Should we go?"

"Let's eat, and then if it starts, we'll head home."

The potluck buffet stretched over two tables with one additional table, nearly bowed with its load of desserts. Cassie and Nicky appeared to be warming up to Jenna. Soon, they were teasing each other.

Pete ate a grilled brat and munched tangy, barbecue potato chips while Eleanor ate tuna noodle salad and cherry tomatoes dipped in sour cream and chives. She popped one into his mouth and he recalled the day he'd fed her wild, red raspberries.

The dark storm clouds flew at them, closing out the sun. The wind picked up, carrying away unattended foam plates and tossing Eleanor's long hair around. Lightning flashed; thunder rattled in the distance. They had just discarded their foam plates and cups when the first drops descended. He picked up Cassie while Eleanor ran with Nicky and Jenna, holding their hands. By the time the pickup doors had been slammed, thunder crashed above them.

Picnickers flocked to their cars and pickups. The Paxtons raced past toward their van.

Jenelle, almost nine months pregnant, waddled more than ran. Pete sat back listening to the rain pelt the roof. He didn't start the engine. Too many children were running around unattended, and he didn't want to make the mistake of not seeing one.

"I wish we could go home and swing on the swing set," Cassie said, sounding deflated.

"The sun will come out again," Eleanor said. "We had fun, didn't we?"

"Yeah, but I'm tired of all this rain," Nicky said.

"Me, too," Pete agreed.

"Let's sing *Itsy Bitsy Spider,*" Eleanor suggested. She put her fingers together and began singing and moving her fingers like spider legs.

Pete joined in and then the kids began making the hand motions. A few minutes later, Pete felt it was safe to start the drive home. Even with another storm they didn't need— what a day, a good day. Their first day together, all five of them.

Pete had expected to be able to fall asleep easily, but he couldn't turn his mind off. Images of Eleanor flitted through his thoughts. Finally, he gave up and went downstairs for a glass of milk.

The phone rang.

He glanced at the clock. Nearly 11:00 p.m. An emergency? He warily lifted the receiver off the wall. "Hello, this is the Beck house."

"Pete, it's me. Suzann."

Chapter Twelve

Pete didn't know how long he stood mute, too stunned, too shaken to speak.

"Pete? Are you there?"

"Why are you calling me?" Hot anger shoved shock aside. His voice came out low and harsh, hurting his throat.

"I know you don't want to hear from me, but I had to call."

"Why?" he spat out the word, his heart pounding in his ears.

"I'm older." Her voice sounded controlled and neutral as if she'd written this out or rehearsed it. "And have had time to think over what happened between us."

"So?" *Do I care?*

"I'm not calling because I want to change the custody arrangement between us or anything like that, but I don't think it's good for our children—"

Fury slashed him. "Don't call them that. You didn't want them four years ago. You don't get to call them *your* children."

Silence. "I expected you to be angry. But I'm not a monster. I was never meant to be a full-time mother, and I don't have the patience motherhood needs, but I don't think it's good for Cassandra and Nicholas to think that I rejected them."

His heart congealed. "You did reject them." *And me.*

"I couldn't handle being a mom," Suzann's carefully controlled voice continued. "I was overwhelmed, and I think I was suffering from postpartum depression."

"You might recall at the time," he added sarcastically, "I asked you to consider that you might be depressed."

"I know. I made a lot of poor decisions. But I don't want our children to suffer the rest of their lives because I wasn't up to being their mother."

How long did it take you to think of them, not yourself? "What do you want?" he asked shortly, arming himself against her.

"I don't know, really. I want you to think about how I can be a long-distance mother. May I send cards or presents? May I visit every year and see the kids?"

Pete wanted to slam the receiver down, but

he held himself back from acting rashly. This wasn't just about him. Cassie and Nicky were what mattered. "I'll have to think about this, Suzann." Each word cost him; perspiration dotted his forehead. "And there's someone in my life now."

"Oh, I see." Suzann's voice trailed off. "But that's good, right? I wasn't meant to be married, but you were."

Hot words of recrimination boiled up from deep inside Pete. He choked them down. "Is that all, Suzann?"

"Yes, that's all. I'll just leave it at that...till you contact me."

"Goodbye." He hung up before he heard her farewell. Still boiling with fury and hurt, he suddenly felt weak at the knees. He braced his hands flat against the kitchen wall, trying to keep his world from spinning out of control. Why did she have to call now?

The next afternoon, just after lunch, a still groggy Pete shuffled out of the kitchen. He hoped he didn't look as bad as he felt. He'd barely slept at all last night. Thoughts of Suzann, painful memories of his months of caring for his colicky Cassie, bewildered Nicky, whom their own mother didn't want, swarmed around in his mind.

He walked toward the barn to let his dad know that he had to go to school for a meeting with the principal.

The barn doors flapped open. His dad stalked outside. "I need to talk to you."

Then Harry led Pete back into the kitchen and waited for Pete to join him, glaring down at the tiny, gray kitten mewing up at him from the wide-plank floor.

The helpless animal and his father's anger over something so slight made Pete lose his temper. "It's just a kitten," he snapped. "You should be thankful every day that you married our mom instead of sniping at her."

"What's got into you?" Harry snapped in return.

"Suzann called last night." Pete slumped into a kitchen chair, depleted by his flash of anger.

His dad gawked at him and then sat down across from him. "It's just as well. That's what I wanted to talk to you about."

"What?" Pete couldn't believe what his dad was saying.

"Suzann calling should be a good reminder to you," his dad scolded. "You've gone and done the same thing again."

"What?"

"You've fallen for another career woman. You

even picked out another lawyer, for goodness' sake. What are you thinking?"

Disbelief vibrating in waves through him, Pete stared at his dad. "Eleanor is not Suzann."

His dad humphed loud and long. "So you think."

"Eleanor is not Suzann," Pete repeated. But in his fatigue and upset, he recognized that Eleanor was outwardly like his ex-wife.

"Eleanor's a career woman. And look at her own mother. Has about as much warmth in her heart as an ice cube. The apple doesn't fall far from the tree."

"Dad—"

Harry talked over him. "You can bet on that. When push comes to shove, *Ms.* Eleanor Washburn will put her career before you and your kids—just the way their mom did in Las Vegas. You mark my words." With that, his dad got up and stalked from the room.

Pete gripped the table edge as if it were a lifeline. He knew his dad would always take the worst view of anything. He was the perennial naysayer, the grump. But the poisoned barbs had shot straight into Pete's tender spot.

What if I am making the same mistake?

Ellie isn't Suzann.

But can I be sure? Will she devote herself to Cassie, Nicky and Jenna? That's a tall order.

Well, I'll be there, too. We'll be working together taking care of the kids. I have more time off and more flexibility with my teaching job.

So I already know that I'll be the main parent?

No. Ellie loves the kids and already adjusts her schedule for them and for others.

Pete rubbed his taut forehead. These upsetting thoughts had tied his neck muscles in knots, too. He wanted to believe that in the future he and Ellie could make it, make a blended family work. But the statistics were stacked against them.

Pete released the table and bent his head. "Dear Lord," he prayed out loud. "What should I do? Would Ellie and I make it as a couple? Or will it end in disaster, like my first marriage? I want to do what's right, what's best for all of us, Nicky, Cassie and Jenna, too. Help me. Help us."

Another front was approaching later that day. Returning from a longer than expected discussion with the principal, Pete arrived home from school and went out looking for his kids to bring them inside before the next storm arrived.

Since Pete had awakened later than usual and then been called to school to discuss some plans for the house to be built this year, his normal schedule with the kids had been upset. As usual, his family had taken up the slack.

Blocking the memory of his dad's corrosive words, Pete expected to find the kids on the playset and headed straight to it. Empty. If they weren't there, they'd be with one of his parents. He walked to the ancient, red barn with its stone foundation. His youngest brother, Landon, and his dad were fixing a tractor engine in the late-afternoon sun in the open doorway. When he joined them, he heard Nicky up in the loft, playing with the litter of barn kittens.

Passing by Landon and Harry, Pete climbed up the ladder, expecting to see Cassie with her brother. He scanned the hayloft. "Hey, Nick, where's your sister?"

Nicky lay on his back with a kitten in each hand, rubbing their noses together. He rolled to the side and put one kitten down gently. "After lunch, we were playing on the playset. She went in the house to get you."

"When did she go into the house?"

"Right after lunch. We saw you go into the kitchen with grandpa." Nicky tickled the kitten under its tiny chin.

A sudden suspicion squeezed Pete's lungs. "But Cassie didn't come in then." He hoped against hope that his daughter hadn't overheard the conversation with his father.

Nicky shrugged and then trailed a bit of red yarn in front of the kittens. "She said that's what she was going to do."

"And you haven't seen her since?"

Nicky shook his head emphatically no.

Pete lowered himself down rung by rung, but his heart had sped up. They lived in the country, their farm set far back from the lane. The kids had a playset and the barn and three adults to oversee them. When he'd left, his brother had said that he was watching Cassie and Nicky. But sometimes, the kids forgot to let the nearest adult know that they were going to another place to play on the farm. The children knew their limits and had never crossed them. And as long as they stayed away from any of the machinery, the farm was a safe place for them.

Pete reached the dusty barn floor. Through the open doors, he glimpsed the cattle out in the pasture, grazing happily. His dad and brother were clanging tools and arguing about something—the usual. A tiny spark of fear flickered to life. He quelled it. The kids had a habit of finding places to get distracted and linger in— just like he and his brothers had when they were kids here. He headed toward the propped-open barn doors. "Dad! Landon! Have you seen Cassie?"

They both looked up. Perhaps the sharp tone

of his voice alerted them. They looked at each other and then his dad replied, "I saw her outside the kitchen this morning after we...after we talked about that woman."

At the words *that woman* Landon looked at Pete questioningly.

Pete shook his head, letting his brother know he wouldn't be discussing that now. As a reminder that "little pitchers have big ears," as his mother would say, Pete gave a toss of his head toward Nicky in the barn loft. "Nicky says he hasn't seen her since then, either."

"Cassie isn't on the playset?" Landon asked.

Pete shook his head. "Another storm's on the way."

As if on cue, the weather radio in the corner crackled to life with a forecast. The three men listened to a storm warning that included strong winds, lightning and a possibility of hail. Pete's fear ratcheted up another notch.

Harry put down the wrench he was holding. "I'll call your mother. She's at the church, some planning committee meeting. Maybe she took Cassie with her." His dad headed toward the house at a trot.

Landon came over to Pete and laid a reassuring hand on his shoulder. "Where should I look?"

"I don't know." Pete lifted both hands, his

stomach swaying and swishing with cold fear. *Don't jump to conclusions. Kids do this stuff.*

"Do you think she'd be down at the creek?" Landon asked.

"She never goes there without Nicky or me." Pete shoved his hands into his pockets.

"Why don't you check in all the farm buildings?" Landon suggested. "And I'll look over the pasture and run down to the creek."

Pete nodded, not having any better plan. "Nicky!" he called up. "Stay in the loft. A storm's coming. If your sister comes in here, tell her to stay with you and the kittens!"

"Okay, Dad!" Nicky called back, sounding unconcerned.

Pete ran out of the barn and headed to one of the many machine sheds. Nothing much to do there, and without windows, they were dark and unwelcoming. The kids hardly ever went in there, especially Cassie.

Still, he opened each, calling, "Cassie! Cassie! Storm's coming!" He crouched low, looking under the old farm machinery, and climbed up to look over it. No Cassie. After searching each one, he met Landon coming back from the pasture.

His brother shook his head no. "Maybe she's inside in her room, reading or something?"

The two of them ran into the kitchen. Harry

met them there. "She's not in the house. Your mom's on her way back. I also checked out front in the ditch along the lane." He shook his head negatively.

All the usual places investigated, Pete's worry zoomed to fear, full-out and raging. "Where do you think she might have gone?" The horrifying thought that someone might have snatched her reared its ghastly head.

As if reading his mind, Harry said, "The kids never go near the lane, and our place's not near any main road, not even a county one. Who would even drive all the way back here?"

Pete weighed this, gripping the frayed ends of his calm. It made sense, but where was Cassie?

His mom's SUV lurched to a halt outside the back door and she sailed in. "Have you found her?"

The men's expressions must have been enough to tell her the bad news. "Have you checked under all the beds? She might have crawled under and fallen asleep."

The men took off, each running to a different bedroom. Soon they all arrived back downstairs. On her knees, his mother was peering under the sofa and chairs. She got up from her knees. "I checked all the hidey-holes in the cellar. And she's not under any of the furniture on the first floor."

"Nor any of the beds," Harry said, looking even more sour than usual.

"I shouldn't have slept in this morning," Pete said, guilt riddling him.

"Nonsense." His mother dismissed this with a wave of her hand. "Kids do these things. How do you think I got these gray hairs? Now, can anybody think of a reason that Cassie might have left the farm?"

Pete hesitated and then said, with a glance at his dad, "Nicky says that she came to the house when she saw me getting coffee in the kitchen."

"I didn't see her," Harry said, looking disgruntled.

"Nicky said she came to the kitchen," his mother repeated slowly, studying both him and Harry. "Did something happen in the kitchen this morning while I was away?"

Pete and his dad exchanged unhappy glances.

"You tell her," his dad said.

Pete began, "I was late getting up because Suzann called me last night—"

"Why did Suzann call?" Kerry Ann asked, not sounding happy.

"She wants…she wants to know if she can send the kids gifts and come to visit them once a year."

"Good of her." His dad sneered. "Generous."

Kerry Ann gave him a sideways look. "You can't get blood from a turnip."

"Exactly." His dad appeared to swell with indignation. "I told Pete he's doing it all over again. That Eleanor Washburn isn't the right kind of woman for him. Another lady lawyer."

His mother propped her hands on her hips and said with palpable indignation, "Eleanor is not Suzann. Anybody could see that."

Harry folded his arms and glared at the world in general. "That's your opinion."

Shaking her head to indicate disagreement with Harry, Kerry Ann looked at Pete. "You've looked in all the obvious places on the farm?"

"Yes," Pete said. Landon and Harry nodded.

"Then, you all comb the places that aren't obvious and—" She broke off as Pete's son appeared in the kitchen doorway. "Nicky, we can't find your sister. Do you have any idea where she would be?"

"No, Grandma. She went to ask Dad if she could have a friend over and I stayed on the playset."

Kerry Ann held out her hand. "Very well. You come stay with me, and we'll start calling our friends." Nicky obeyed, heading toward his grandmother.

"But, Mom," Pete objected. "She wouldn't have left the farm."

With Nicky holding her hand, Kerry Ann glanced over her shoulder. "She might, if she was upset." She pressed her lips together. "We'll find her. Don't start thinking the worst. And pray!"

Pete wanted to argue, wanted to yell in frustration and helpless rage.

"Don't worry," his dad said with an attempt at heartiness. "We'll find her."

"Yeah," Landon agreed. "Let's try to think like a little girl. Where would I go if I were unhappy?"

Holding it all in, Pete closed his eyes. *Dear Lord, where's my daughter?*

"Eleanor," Kerry Ann's voice came over the phone, sounding urgent. "We can't find Cassie."

Eleanor stood in the room that would be Jenna's. She wore her paint clothes, and Mavis knelt nearby masking the baseboards.

"You can't find Cassie?" Eleanor repeated.

"We think she overheard Pete and his dad talking about her mother calling from Las Vegas last night."

Why would Pete's ex call? And what had been said that upset Cassie? Was Pete's ex trying to come back into his life?

"Cassie's missing?" Mavis asked, rising, her knees creaking.

"Yes." Eleanor spoke into the phone again. "What can we do?"

"I think it's possible that Cassie might try to go to your house. Under the circumstances." Kerry Ann emphasized the last phrase.

"But we live over two miles from you. Would Cassie know the way?"

"Yes, fortunately or unfortunately, you live on the way to the public pool and baseball diamond. We always wave at your house as we pass. And that's been a few times a week this summer."

"What can we do?" Mavis asked, her ear now on the other side of the receiver, close to Eleanor.

"Would you please drive slowly toward our place?" Kerry Ann asked. "I'm setting out from our place to another house. And so are Pete, Harry and Landon, to different destinations. We're trying to cover the routes to every house Cassie would be able to find on her own. Storm's coming fast."

"Okay." Thunder rumbled ominously. They exchanged cell phone numbers and hung up.

"We'll take my car," Mavis said, already running down the hall toward the back door. She snatched up her purse from a kitchen chair.

Eleanor ran right behind her, grabbing her purse from its hook in the back hall and slamming the door behind her. "I won't lock it in case we miss Cassie and she gets here before we get back!"

"Good idea!" Mavis folded herself behind the wheel and Eleanor jumped into the passenger seat. Lightning streaked overhead.

"I'll drive," Mavis commanded. "You look and pray!"

Eleanor began a silent chant. "Please, Lord, let Cassie be safe. Let someone find her. Keep her safe."

Mavis's bright red hybrid crept down the road with Eleanor scanning both sides. The rain poured down, nearly defeating the flapping windshield wipers. Looking out through the veil of pouring rain made Eleanor feel like she was drowning.

She opened the window a crack, raindrops flying inside, and began calling, "Cassie! Cassie!"

The thunder swallowed her pathetic voice. Her inward chant became a ribbon of words, of worry. In that moment, she knew without a doubt that she loved Cassie as much as if she were her own flesh. *God, keep her safe. Please. Don't let anything bad happen to her.*

Eleanor pinned her intense gaze on the road, alternately switching from one side to the other. The distance between her house and the Beck farm had never seemed as long before.

Then Mavis slammed on the brakes. "There! Under those oak trees!" Cassie was huddled under the thrashing branches. "Oh, no, the worst place for her!"

Stopping Mavis by gripping her arm, Eleanor said, "I'll go." She tossed Mavis her cell phone. "Call Kerry Ann!"

She burst out of the car. The deluge soaked her to the skin. "Cassie!" she screamed, the effort scoring her throat. *"Cassie!"*

Suddenly the thunder became uninterrupted, pounding, throbbing, deafening. Lighting streaked around them, stunningly bright. Cassie ran toward her. Eleanor raced to her, her arms outstretched. She felt herself still screaming, "Cassie!" But couldn't hear anything save the thunder.

Cassie lunged into her arms, shaking with sobs. Eleanor lifted her and ran toward the car, the safest place in a lightning storm. In the maelstrom, she glimpsed Pete's pickup zooming up the road toward Mavis's car. *Pete, help!*

The world exploded. Eleanor was slammed to the earth, still clutching Cassie. Burning debris fell around them, hitting Eleanor as she shielded Cassie under her. She felt herself screaming into the maelstrom. *Lord! Help! Pete! Help!*

Something hard and heavy hit her shoulder. It burned. She turned and saw that her shoulder was aflame. Before she could react, rain doused the orange fire. And then on the top of her head—a blow. *Oh!* She slumped, lost consciousness.

Chapter Thirteen

Eleanor swam upward from some dark, silent place. She tried to open her eyes, but the light around her was painfully bright.

"Eleanor, Ellie." A familiar voice repeated her name over and over. She knew that voice.

She forced herself to open her eyes a tiny bit. Pete stood over her, repeating her name.

"Pete?" she whispered, relief shining through her as if she were transparent. That's how she felt thin, transparent, ready to blow away.

"Ellie?" He gripped her hand tighter. "Ellie, wake up."

"I'm awake," she whispered, bringing his distraught face into focus. Something had sprinkled her body with pain. "What happened?"

Her simple words seemed to unleash a torrent of words.

"What were you thinking?" Pete demanded.

"You could have been killed. I could have lost you! And Cassie! Don't you ever go out in a storm like that again."

She could feel his hand shaking even as it clutched hers.

"I could have lost both of you," he repeated and fell silent. He lifted her hand to his lips and kissed it. "Ellie, I nearly died when I saw you running in the rain and then...the lightning..." he murmured brokenly.

"Cassie?" she asked, still unable to lift her voice above a whisper.

"She's fine." His voice shook. "Just soaking wet and scared."

A memory pricked her and burning pain sparked a grimace. "My shoulder?"

"You have first degree burns on your shoulder, and smaller ones, dotting various other places. One of the oak trees behind you took a direct lightning strike and exploded around you. You could have been hurt really bad, Ellie. Really bad."

"Had to. Cassie...under the oak trees. Worst place," Eleanor replied, straining to make herself heard. "Saw you, too."

"I should have gotten there first," he said.

"Where's my daughter?" A loud voice from somewhere beyond Pete intruded.

Then her mother and father bustled to her other side.

"Eleanor," her mother exclaimed. "You look awful. Mavis told us what you did. If the tree had been any closer, you could have been killed." Her mother burst into tears and covered her face with her hands.

Eleanor watched, too stunned to speak.

Her father lifted Eleanor's free hand and squeezed it. "If you hadn't gotten Cassie out from under that tree, she could have been killed. That's my girl."

Her mother turned her face into John's shoulder, obviously still shaking with tears.

Pete squeezed Eleanor's hand again. "My sweet, brave Ellie." He tried to smile but his chin still trembled.

"Want to see Miss Ellie!" Cassie ran into the room, followed by Kerry Ann who caught up with her and lifted her into her arms.

"Well, Eleanor," Kerry Ann said, "looks like you're going to make it. See, Cassie, Miss Ellie is going to be fine."

"Pardon me," a white-coated doctor edged into the E.R. examining area. "I know you're all concerned about the patient, but I need all but one of you to go out to the waiting area. In fact, how did you all get by the receptionist?" He looked accusingly at each of them in turn.

"Come along, Delia," John coaxed. "We'll go sit in the waiting room. We can fuss over our girl when we get her home," he said, and departed.

"That will be very soon," the doctor said. "We just need to watch her to see if she shows any sign of concussion. Otherwise, she has only suffered scattered first degree burns and minor lacerations. She'll be fine."

The crowd ebbed, but Pete remained, gripping her hand. He listened also as the doctor finished his assessment of her and then told her that she would be there for a few more hours of observation. He prescribed a pain reliever.

When they were alone again, Pete leaned down and kissed her. "Now I'm going to talk to Mavis about my bringing fresh clothing for you from home. What you were wearing was mud-smeared, drenched and singed."

"I always try to look my best," Eleanor said, lowering her eyelids demurely.

Pete laughed out loud and it felt good to expand his lungs, release his anxiety. "You look beautiful. Always." He leaned down and stole another kiss. "But I know you'll feel better in clean clothes."

Later Eleanor sat in a wheelchair, and Pete pushed her out to the exit, her family and his following, too. It wasn't long before they were all gathered in Eleanor's living room. Kerry Ann had brought Cassie, too.

With Eleanor safely at home, Pete found he could finally breathe normally. Eleanor had refused to lie down and sat in a comfortable armchair in her beige-and-white living room in her blue, cotton robe and matching slippers. He sat on the wide arm of the comfortable, overstuffed tweed chair, needing to be touching her. Her parents also remained, hovering close.

Mavis motioned toward the work clothing she wore as she sank into another armchair. "We were going to paint Jenna's room. She chose a pale peach shade last weekend."

The commonplace words somehow released the tension in the room. Cassie climbed onto John's lap, sighed and almost instantly collapsed into deep sleep.

"Too much excitement," John said, stroking Cassie's tear-streaked face.

Delia reached over and also touched the child's hair and face. "I'm so glad she wasn't hurt. Whenever I think of her standing under trees during such a storm..." She shuddered visibly.

"Children push us to the edge," Kerry Ann agreed, sounding exhausted.

"I remember when, as a child, Eleanor was hit by a car while she was riding her bike,"

Delia said, her eyes on Cassie. "I couldn't stay in the hospital room, I was crying so hard. I was terrified by the fact that we could have lost her."

Pete watched Eleanor's face turn pink. He squeezed her hand.

"I remember," Eleanor murmured. "Dad told me you were out in the hall calling your office."

"That's what she told me to tell you," John said.

"I didn't want my tears to weaken you. You had to be strong," Delia said, her voice firming.

Eleanor wiped away a tear, suddenly feeling light enough to rise from where she sat and hover near the ceiling. *My mother loves me, has always loved me—in her way.* "I'm just glad I found Cassie in time. And no real harm done. The doctor said my injuries will heal up in a week."

"You got off light," Pete said, the thought of the possible tragedy evidently still shaking him.

Eleanor sighed, leaning her head back against the soft chair. "All's well that ends well. And thank goodness I don't have to appear in court anytime soon." She glanced down at the burns and cuts that were scattered over her arms and hands.

Kerry Ann rose. "I'm going into the kitchen to get Ellie something to eat and drink. And then I think we should all go home—except for Pete—and let Eleanor get some rest." She walked out of the room before anyone could react to her announcement.

John lifted an eyebrow. "Should I be asking you about your intentions, young man?"

Pete snorted. "I'm not that young. But I am wiser, this time. Eleanor and I have an understanding about the future, don't we?"

Eleanor nodded but looked sleepy.

"Eleanor and I are going to take our time to do this right," Pete continued. "She's going to be in the process of adopting Jenna, and we need to plan our course so that our blended family comes together with tender care."

Pete was glad that no one here had asked why Cassie had run out into the storm. He didn't want to reveal this before he discussed it privately with Eleanor.

Kerry Ann returned from the kitchen. "I've put some lasagna I found in the freezer into the oven and have set the timer. When it dings, Pete, be sure to get it out." Kerry Ann then lifted Cassie, carrying her toward the door and shooing the rest of the gathering out the door. Waving farewell, Pete didn't move from the arm of the chair close to Eleanor.

When they were alone, Eleanor asked, "Why did Cassie run away?"

Pete pressed his lips together for a moment. The anger he felt at Suzann flared and then began to ebb. Eleanor rested against his arm. That's what counted now. "She overheard my dad warning me away from you. My ex, Suzann, called last night."

"After four years of nothing?" Eleanor was flabbergasted. What nerve!

"After not even sending a Christmas card in all these years." Pete nodded glumly. "She has finally come to the realization that she has children. And that her actions have affected them. She wants to figure out how to be a long-distance mom."

"How does one do that?" Eleanor touched Pete's cheek, needing to be in contact with this man, this man she loved so.

"She suggested sending presents and coming for a visit every year." His expression and tone were dry.

"What do you think of that?" Eleanor stroked his cheek with the back of her hand.

He shrugged. "I guess we should let her. The kids should know their birth mother. I know they wonder why she stayed in Las Vegas and we live here. I've never come up with an adequate reason for that—one that I could tell them."

Eleanor nodded pensively but again her heart lightened. "You said 'we.' I'm glad."

He drew her hand up to his lips to press another kiss there. "And I'm sorry. After I told my dad about Suzann's call, he made me doubt you—for about three seconds. Then I remembered that he doesn't approve of anything or anybody at first. He likes you. He just worries a lot." Pete paused. "He has reason I guess. My marrying Suzann ended up hurting not only my children but also my whole family."

"That can't be helped. 'Sufficient unto the day is the evil thereof,'" she recited.

He nodded as he leaned over to steal a kiss. "Yes, just living through today's drama and trauma is definitely enough."

"I don't really understand what kind of woman your ex is. And I love Nicky and Cassie already."

"I know. I see it in the way you look at them, your tone of voice. You talk to them like a mom. And you love Jenna, too."

"I want to be a good mom like Mavis was to me." Eleanor wondered if she'd seen and heard right. "Did my mother really come in and cry over me?"

He grinned, nodding. "Yeah, she did."

"I never thought she loved me." Eleanor still felt disoriented. Too much had transpired in much too short of a time. She was glad she didn't have to do anything but sit.

"She just has a funny way of showing it," Pete said. "Like my dad."

"Guess we'll just have to take them as they come," Eleanor said, grinning wryly, feeling old chains of doubt fall away, crumble, disappear. If only she weren't so tired and achy. Pain leaked through the pills they gave her at the hospital. She sighed.

"We have to accept our families the way they love us—"

"And vice versa. Our kids will have to take us as we are." She leaned against Pete's solid form.

"Just like God loves us and all his children. No matter what. You are a very special woman and I love you."

At this revelation, she glanced up. His eyes spoke not of kindness and friendship, but of love. Joy filled her so that she couldn't speak. Instead, she stroked his cheek with her index finger.

He turned and kissed the inside of her palm. "I love you, Eleanor," he repeated, grinning. "Ellie."

His voice caressed her and she closed her eyes. "I love you, too, Pete." Her voice betrayed her by squeaking at the end.

He chuckled as if she'd said something uproarious and lowered his mouth to claim hers again. She let herself ride the wave of the kiss and then sighed. "I can't believe it's real. How did all our fears of loving again disappear? How could everything change in one day?"

"God used a lightning bolt to wake us up. We must really be dense," Pete teased. This time he drew her gently up to stand against him, his arms around her, and then he was kissing her again. She lost herself in the moment, not trying to figure out where her lips ended and his began, and certainly not denying that she wanted Pete Beck to kiss her.

Finally he ended the kiss. She rested her head on his chest, comforted by his racing, thudding heart under her ear. Gently he urged her back into her chair. "After you eat, I'll stay till you go to bed. If you need me, just call."

She rested her head against him, not feeling the need to reply. Words weren't necessary.

Pete gently stroked her hair, and the two of them found peace in silence together. Eleanor thought she had aged about twenty years today, but all that mattered was that everyone was safe. And loved.

Nearly a month later Pete carried one end of a sofa into the Paxtons' finished Habitat house.

Jenelle and Kevan were moving in today. The volunteers called out cheerful encouragement to each other. Pete's own joy bubbled up and burst forth in an easy laughter and an unquenchable smile.

Eleanor appeared to be filled with the same exuberance. Kevan and Jenelle glowed with happiness, and little Tiesha couldn't stop hopping and singing. Uncle Dex kept busy carrying in boxes, high-fiving everybody in sight. He'd decided to take his nephew up on his offer to rent a suite in the basement. Or the future suite. Pete had offered to help Kevan put in a second bathroom along with a bedroom in the basement. Luis and Colby had offered to help, too.

A delivery truck from the local furniture store lurched to a noisy stop in front of the Paxton house. The first two families to receive Habitat houses—Rosa and Marc Chambers and their son Johnny, and Jeannie and Jake McClure and their twin girls—all shouted with delight.

Pete looked around, a bit confused.

The driver stalked toward them, looking disgruntled, plainly put out. "I have another anonymous delivery to make here. For the third time. Who are the Paxtons?"

Eleanor burst into laughter, and many others joined her. "Let me guess. You have a bedroom set for the Paxtons?"

"Yeah. Now, am I going to have to stand here and argue with you people, or can my guy and me just get the set inside?"

Kevan and Jenelle looked confused. "But we didn't—"

Rosa Chambers rushed to them. "It happened to both of us, too." She gestured toward the McClure clan. "On our moving-in days, a bedroom set was delivered from an anonymous donor."

"Lady," the delivery man moaned, "I just want to deliver and get on with my day!"

At this, the crowd laughed even louder. The driver looked ready to explode.

"Please," Eleanor said for the still-dazed Paxtons. "Bring the furniture right in."

Within short order, a lovely, walnut bedroom set filled the master bedroom. The delivery men waved without looking back, and their truck soon left with a grinding of gears.

Kevan and Jenelle stood in the doorway of their bedroom.

"This is the nicest furniture I've ever owned," Jenelle whispered.

Kevan leaned down and kissed her. "I told you we'd love living away from the city."

Eleanor whispered in Pete's ear. "My dad is the secret benefactor. He told me this morning that he did it because he wanted to support my work on these three projects, and he couldn't be here till just recently."

Pete barely digested this.

Then Jenelle exclaimed with surprise, "Oh! Oh!" She ran for the bathroom and then called through the door. "Kevan, I'm in labor! Bring me some dry clothes!"

There was a rush to paw through the clothing boxes, and then Kevan and Jenelle were heading off toward the hospital. Tiesha clung to Mavis and Kerry Ann's hands, looking concerned.

Mavis stooped down. "Now don't you worry about your mama. The doctors and nurses will take good care of her."

"That's right," Dex added. "And Aunt Mavis and I will take care of you."

Kerry Ann also stooped. "Yes, and before you know it, you'll have a new brother or sister."

"I'm getting a new sister. She's named Jenna," Cassie piped up. "When my daddy marries Miss Ellie."

The volunteers gathered around Pete and Eleanor with congratulations. The men pounded Pete's back, and the women asked if a date had been set. Pete pulled Eleanor close under his arm. She basked in the genuine affection and joy from these good friends.

Epilogue

The day of Pete's parents' fortieth-wedding-anniversary party came the following weekend. Pete couldn't tell if his mother had guessed or heard about the surprise for them. His dad, however, was completely astonished and couldn't stop grinning. A coup if there ever was one.

The grounds behind the Island City Lake Resort abounded with the Beck clan and countless old friends. Jenelle and Kevan had brought their brand-new son, Vincent, along with big sister, Tiesha, and Uncle Dex. Danny Miller and Mike stood under a tree, looking smug. They'd just won the db Drag Racing World Championship. Pete chuckled to himself. The Becks were a family filled with individuals.

Eleanor came and slipped her arm into his. "It's time to cut the cake." They walked to join his parents at the long table draped with a spotless, white tablecloth, compliments of the resort. A vast sheet cake, decorated with daisies, his mother's favorite flower, nearly covered the table.

His parents stood behind the cake, suffering all the people snapping pictures of them. His mother wore one of her long summer dresses, and his dad was in his usual special-occasion, crisp, white dress shirt and black slacks.

Just before his mother ceremonially cut the first piece of cake, she looked archly at Pete. "Don't you have an announcement to make?"

He grinned, really wanting to dance around the cake with his own happiness. He pulled Eleanor to his side and motioned Nicky, Cassie and Jenna to stand in front of them. "Eleanor and I would like to officially announce our engagement."

He lifted her hand, displaying the vintage ring which had belonged to his great-grandmother. Suzann had refused it, wanting a modern ring. Eleanor, of course, had been deeply touched by the family connection and had loved it on sight. "We have set the date for next August on this same day!"

The last of his words were overwhelmed by applause and shouts of praise and encouragement. Someone tapped a glass with a spoon. Pete obliged by pulling Eleanor close and kissing her. Jenna, Nicky and Cassie crowded around them, smiling and laughing.

Sufficient unto the day is the evil thereof. And sometimes the joy. Another person, then many people, tapped their glasses. He kissed Eleanor again. And then pulled her away.

"Cut the cake, Mother! I want to kiss Eleanor in private."

Gales of laughter cascaded around them. He kept Eleanor at his side, and all three children stood in front of them. He rested a hand on Jenna's shoulder and Eleanor rested one on Nicky's.

In light of her own lonely childhood, at the beginning of this summer, she'd doubted her ability to love a child. But over the past three months her heart had expanded because of Pete Beck. Now she loved a good man, his son and daughter, and Jenna. The more love she gave, the more she found she could give. Love didn't divide; it multiplied. It was a wonder, a miracle. Her heart sang as she affectionately squeezed Nicky's—her future son's—shoulder.

Then she turned her face and Pete began kissing her. She didn't pull away despite shyness at kissing in front of all these people. A chuckle formed in her throat as she listened to their friends' and families' loud approval—wolf whistles, applause and shouts of encouragement. And why not? They were building a family together—with God's help.

* * * * *

Dear Reader,

I hope you enjoyed the three books in this NEW FRIENDS STREET series. I've loved creating these families who are facing the problems that are so common in our society today. Building a family takes work and dedication and love. If we depend solely on our own strength, we can fail. God's love and power can overcome our faults and ease their consequences.

That's one of the best parts of belonging to God. We know He is in charge of today and tomorrow. And had forgiven us for any mistakes we made yesterday.

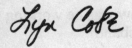

Questions for Discussion

1. Why did Eleanor think her mother didn't love her?

2. Is it ever possible to know for sure what another person's motives are? If so, how?

3. Have you ever known a couple like Kerry Ann and Harry, complete opposites? Do opposites really attract? And is that good?

4. Have you ever tried some new food? If so, what?

5. Kevan was a veteran. How was he working to be a good dad and husband?

6. Have you ever known a free spirit like Kerry Ann? Why do you think some people can always look on the sunny side of the street?

7. What do you think Pete should have said to Suzann that he didn't say? Or did he handle it just right?

LARGER-PRINT BOOKS!

**GET 2 FREE
LARGER-PRINT NOVELS
PLUS 2 FREE
MYSTERY GIFTS**

Larger-print novels are now available...

Love Inspired®
SUSPENSE
RIVETING INSPIRATIONAL ROMANCE

Watch for our series of edge-
of-your-seat suspense novels.
These contemporary tales
of intrigue and romance
feature Christian characters
facing challenges to their faith...
and their lives!

AVAILABLE IN REGULAR
& LARGER-PRINT FORMATS

For exciting stories that reflect traditional values,
visit:
www.ReaderService.com